How Could I Not See Him?

notionpress.com

How Could I Not See Him?

EISHITA

notionpress.com

Notion Press

Old No. 38, New No. 6

McNichols Road, Chetpet

Chennai - 600 031

First Published by Notion Press 2015

ISBN 978-93-5206-430-4

TO

My late grandmother Mrs. Bimla Shukla
who has been in my eyes the human version of
An Iron Lady, and has inspired me a lot.
I love you Dadi and miss you a lot...

Preface

Hello, I am Eishita, the author of the book you are holding in your hands right now. I am a die-hard fan of 'One Direction', Durjoy Datta books and Shahid Kapoor. 'The Fault in Our Stars', 'Hold My Hand', 'Till the Last Breath', 'I Too Had A Love Story' and 'Can Love Happen Twice?' are some of my favorite books. This is the first among my books to be published.

I wrote this book when I was thirteen. A few pessimistic people had predicted that I would prove to be useless. I swore to prove them wrong one day. Maybe I have done that. Another inspiration to start writing was because I wanted to bestow something upon my late grandmother and make my parents proud, and because of the urge in myself to become an author ever since I discovered my writing skills. I am not much of a serious person by nature. Therefore, I did not have any specific objectives or goals while writing this book, other than that my story should be read by lots of people. Nonetheless, it is a great feeling to have the tag of 'author' to my name.

Dear Reader, I do hope you will learn from this book to look around and give worth to the right people. The creation of this book was a turning point for me; I have become more sensible and people have started to treat me with the seriousness that I believe I deserved. This book for me is like the first child of a parent, that child who radically alters the parents' lives and makes them ready for the arrival of their future children. "How Could I Not See Him?" is like my first child. I am thankful to you for buying it, taking out time from your busy schedule and reading it.

I would appreciate if you drop your messages or DMs on Twitter, Instagram and Facebook as soon as you finish reading; I would love to respond to them. I would love it if you please write to me keeping in mind that I am a thirteen year old and that I would not appreciate abusive language. Thank you for buying this and becoming a part of my small family of readers. I hope you like it!

HAPPY READING!

Acknowledgement

I would like to take this moment to express my gratitude to the many people who saw me all the way through this book; to all those who provided support, talked things over, read, wrote, offered comments, allowed me to quote their remarks and to all those who assisted in the editing, proofreading and design. Sorry if I miss out anyone; so many have lent their help unstintingly.

"Being a girl does not mean I will be crushed by men" - the woman who proved this quote was my grandmother. Therefore, this book is a gift to my late grandmother Mrs. Bimla Shukla, the Iron Lady in my life - the real example of bravery, courage and high self-esteem. Thank you for being an inspiration for me to remain strong and keep fighting forever. I love you Dadi!

I would also take this moment to thank my Nanaji, Mr. G.P. Dwivedi, for showering upon me his immense love, support and blessings from up where he resides and belongs to be, paradise.

I would also thank my parents, Pallavi Asheesh and Asheesh Misra, for bringing me into this world, and for their endless support. Without them, I do not think this book would have been where it is today. Thank you for showing your endless support and interest in my work, believing in me and helping me to achieve my dream. I would express my gratitude to my sibling and partner in crime, Aishwarya Di for polishing my English and answering my foolish questions even at midnight.

I would love to thank my friends aka my proofreaders, Priyanshi Mishra, Aanchal Mishra, and Ritika Gaur for encouraging my skills and reading my write ups. I want to put up a special mention to my two best friends and my best proofreaders, Arushi Kanojia and Vidhi Saxena for making me laugh on my lowest days, reading my write ups and obviously tolerating my extremely short temper. Without your help, I do not think I could have made some parts of this book possible. I love you all so much.

And at this moment, I have to thank the Notion Press India Family. Thank you for standing by me through this beautiful phase of book publishing. It has been a great experience with them and their dedicated consultants who have not only designed the cover and edited my book, but also have answered the endless amounts of questions I've bugged them with, even at two or three in the morning.

Last but not the least, I would love to thank Mr. Durjoy Datta, who has always been an endless source of inspiration and information for me. Thank you everyone!

EISHITA...

Prologue

Yuvraj

"He made me open my eyes. He is the best thing that has ever happened to me; amidst all the bad things that I have gone through, he has been by my side, holding me firmly and preventing me from collapsing. He is the one who puts stars in my sky." Aanya flashed her beautiful smile standing on the podium.

"Let me tell you none of all of this started with clichés like 'A prince and a princess'. It started, unlike many, with 'A nerd boy and a hot girl'." I laughed as I spoke in between, waving my hands up in an action of surrender.

"Aanya and Yuvraj, would you like to tell us how you two happened?" the host asked us in a sugar-sweet voice and with her typical heavy British accent.

"I would love it if Yuvraj shares our story with you." She looked at me, flashing her perfect teeth.

"I would love to do it. Just that it is a bit too long. You need to be patient! Come; witness the love story of a nerd boy." I joked and took a deep breath, closing my eyes as our beautiful and romantic story flashed in front of my eyes like a PowerPoint presentation.

Everyone needs at least one opportunity to tell their love story to the world, to share with them the little fights, funs, arguments and the beautiful moments they have shared with their partners. Not all get such opportunities, but I did. Through our hard work and sustained hope, we have made it here and we are proud of it. I took a deep breath and started...

1

Yuvraj

People thought that as I was a topper I had a large number of friends as is usual with topper kids, for sharing notes and everything. However, I was always different; the real fact is that I do not have many friends; in fact, I do not have any friends at all except for my best friend and a girl I have a big crush on. Okay, the real thing is that my best friend is the girl I have a crush on; Aanya is the name she was blessed with sixteen years back.

Aanya Saeed, one of the most beautiful girls of our school, and surprisingly my best friend. Her very long, dark brown, wavy hair ending just above her waist, fair and flawless skin, and the most beautiful, expressive coal-black eyes which are as deep as the ocean, could mesmerize the viewer in a trice. Her eyes in particular could cast a spell that would make anyone drown in them just by a locking stare for a few seconds. Along with her cute and round face, she has an impressive height of five feet and ten inches too, and according to me, she is a somewhat taller version of Alia Bhatt.

She was a stunner, with an angelic and appealing personality, she was classy and sassy and trashy all together with a dazzling, divine and elegant persona. She danced with all determination, energy and abandon which made the audience feel that a peacock was dancing joyously in the rain. She was one who found her happiness in dance, and was easily the best female dancer in school.

The only thing that I did not like about her was her boyfriend, Aarav Singh. He was the kind of boy who would spend a good number of hours in front of the mirror daily. He had big, brown eyes, a tall and masculine physique, not very but short hair, fair skin and loads of girls swooning over his dance moves. Whenever you saw him, he would always be there with his perfectly spiked, gelled hair, very strong AXE deodorant on, and uniform awry in the most horrible way - clothes from Versace or any other big brand. He was the kind of boy you would never see in boxers, but only on GQ or Vogue magazine covers; yes, even at seven in the morning, he was always well dressed.

I would at times see him in black shirt and blue jeans along with his all-time perfect hair, walking on the street, and would change my route because I thought I looked too bad in a grey "Goli nahi marenge sasure ko, keh ke lenge uski" type Gangs of Wasseypur quoted t-shirt from Bewakoof.com along with faded black jeans.

Girls used to compare him with Varun Dhawan of Student Of The Year \ aka Rohan Nanda's character, based on his looks and the heights of being spoiled. He was the only person who dared to be rude to me while Aanya was around.

Coming back to me, I am Yuvraj Thakur Singh, a normal yet topper boy with the average looks of a sixteen-year-old geek. What surprises me most is that my neighbor, Aanchal, says that I look like the international pop sensation Harry Styles from 'One Direction', (if he were to put on glasses), because according to her I have green eyes, fair skin, curly hair, a dimpled smile and a 'masculine' physique together with a great height of six feet. Therefore, I am the "Xerox copy of Harry Styles" (I quote her words). Let me tell you I do not take her seriously even one percent; anyways here am I, a XI standard Commerce student from St. Laurens' Academy, Musoorie, standing in the middle of the corridor and thinking deep.

I pushed my glasses up to my eyes, as I stood in the corridor; the bell rang loudly in a shrill sound, almost making my ears bleed and me deaf. I ran at my fastest pace towards my classroom, as I do not like skipping or being late for classes; being a geek is not easy. Thank God, our class teacher, Mrs. Simantika Kapoor, had not yet made it to the class or I would have been in deep trouble, probably. I went in and sat on the first seat of the third row, right in front of the teacher's table.

Maybe because I am a topper, and therefore a boring person, or maybe because my work is always up-to-date, all the students leave the first seat for me. It astonishes me; I sometimes wonder what would happen if I were to skip school for a day or two, (though, mind you, I never would), but just suppose I were to, who would sit here.

I turned back to spot my best friend and saw a fair girl with braided, long, dark brown hair in a crisp white shirt, navy blue tie, yellow checked skirt ending just above her knees and white socks reaching up to her mid calves - Aanya Saeed.

She was sitting on the last seat with her boyfriend, Aarav Singh - a slightly tanned boy wearing his uniform in the worst possible way, and with hair standing straight up above his forehead. I groaned lightly in my head, as I do not have much of good feelings for him, not because Aanya is dating him or due to something like jealousy; I do not like him because he treats me in the worst possible way - maybe he does not like the special bond that Aanya and I share.

She looked up from her favorite novel "Made For Each Other" by Vanshika Gupta, seemingly bored with the typical "Blah was caught kissing blah" whispered conversations that she dislikes intensely. Her eyes widened as she saw me, and she waved at me, a big smile playing on her lips. I waved back with the same happiness. Aarav noticed it, pulled her hand down, and rolled his eyes at me; she was offended by it, the same as I was, and opened her mouth to say something to me, maybe words of apology; but I turned towards the front. I really wish I could punch Aarav on his face very hard someday or the other.

"Wakey wakey loves!" The class teacher chirped as she entered the class wearing a white sari with black border, minimal makeup and hair up in a tight bun. She was a young twenty-six year old girl, (or maybe woman), with big brown eyes, fair and flawless skin, medium length brown hair, an impressive height of five feet nine inches and a lean figure. She was looking very beautiful that day as always. She clapped to wake up the lazy bees of the class; unlike other class teachers, she was a very friendly woman.

She was one of the most popular young teachers of St. Laurens' Academy who could give any of the present day movie stars like Anushka Sharma, Katrina Kaif and Deepika Padukone a good run for their money. Being the sweetheart she is, she even gives advices - relationship advices and moving on advices - to the girls of her class without spreading them, and allows normal couples to sit together during her class (not the cheesy and irritating ones that cannot keep their hands off each other). People like her because of this but I like her because of her good nature and lenient marking. She is the reason I have been coming out with excellent marks in English from the ninth standard onwards… (For obvious reasons, as I do not have a girlfriend).

"Good morning ma'am," the others sang as they stood up lazily. "Good morning kids, please sit down," she said as she adjusted herself in her chair. "Hello Yuvraj, you have been sitting alone for the last three days?" she asked me. I nodded. "You have no friends?" she asked again. As I tried to stand up, she shook her head as a sign for me to keep sitting.

"I have ma'am, and I don't sit alone usually, my partner is absent today." I smiled as I told her.

"Okay. And who is your friend?" she asked me.

"Ma'am, uh, um, Aan-Aanya Saeed," I looked down.

She looked behind me and nodded, "Aanya come and sit with Yuvraj, fine…just for this class… But do sit here…and Aarav, please mind your own business," she ordered her, while pointing to the seat next to me.

I stood up, "No ma'am, she is sitting wi…"

"It is completely okay! You know I'm quite bored back there," Aanya interrupted me and smiled happily while pointing to the place where she had been sitting earlier, bringing her bag, bottle and a few notebooks. She quickly dumped her stuff next to the bench, kept her things in the desk and sat down. I turned back to see Aarav all red with anger or maybe jealousy at Aanya's response. I tried so hard but could not let my giggle go unnoticed as I found his situation extremely hilarious. "Stop laughing," he mouthed with clenched jaws and furrowed eyebrows but I did not listen, chuckled lightly again just to mock him and turned to the front.

Mrs. Kapoor smiled at me and continued with the class, "Today… I won't teach you guys English," she smiled at the class who were cheering within themselves as the workbooks and assignments had to be submitted and she is very, or I must say only, strict regarding submission of work on time. In addition, let us face it, students of IX standard never do their work in class or even at home. I groaned in my head because I had spent a full week completing my assignment.

"Ale ale Yuvraj! Did your assignment, but Ma'am did not collect? Poor kid!" I heard Aarav yell from the last seat. Ma'am frowned at him, "At least he scores something from those assignments Aarav, unlike you." She pointed at him and looked at the others. "Submit your assignments in the last period, after that I will not take a single file," she announced. Now all the students including Aanya darted death glares on Aarav, while I smirked at him.

"I'm going to announce something you guys would love to know about," she gave a dramatic pause and continued,

"An international dance competition is being held, a couple dance competition..." she again paused to judge the delighted expressions. "International? Oh sure!" Aanya mumbled to herself sarcastically. "Yes Aanya, an 'International Dance Competition' is being held," she smiled at Aanya while making inverted commas in the air. Aanya blessed her with her priceless eye roll.

"And the dance school that is organizing the event will enroll the winning couple in their school. Oh, and the school is...the biggest dance school in London..." she paused and gestured to us to guess the name. "Eternity Dance Troup?" I asked in a high volume due to my eagerness. She nodded sweetly. "Yes, Yuvraj is right, Eternity Dance Troup also known as EDT London," she beamed at the class.

All gasped in utter surprise, shock and delight, as they knew the importance of an admission to Eternity Dance Troup London. Eternity Dance Troup is a London based dance academy and a dazzling dream that every dancer worships from the minute he or she enters the world. Not all get an admission there because firstly the fees are a whopping 1 lakh rupees (in Indian currency); secondly, auditions are held every year all over the world, at the end of which only fifty incredible dancers are enrolled. Once a person is enrolled in Eternity Dance Troup, his life and future are secured fully; their troupes are cast in movies etc. and from these castings, the world is blessed with dancers like Mrs. Manisha Pandey, the noted choreographer of Bollywood, and Mr. Amitesh Sinha, the superstar. One gets to be fully established as a dancer if he gets to be a student of this dance school. The Eternity Dance Troup is the Indian Institute of Technology (also called as IIT) of the dancing world.

"You have to be kidding! The Eternity Dance Troup people are holding a competition here! In Musoorie? This definitely is a rumor, dude! Mad or what are they?" Aanya asked in a super loud tone. Mrs. Simantika chuckled lightly, "Oh God Aanya, relax! Do not give such over elaborated reactions! Let me continue. They are holding the competition in Dehradun, not in Musoorie." She replied as she earned an "Oh" and a nod from Aanya in agreement, instead of the eye roll that she got from her the last time.

I felt her jump happily next to me, and turned to her, "Happy much huh?" I asked her.

"Happy? Watcha thinking boi? I am Excited to death! London, Eternity Dance Troup, Dance, Admission, Aarav, Me!" she drifted off to her own dreamland and I scoffed in my brain at the mention of his name.

"I'm passing the forms to you, if you want to take part, just put up your names and we will fill up the rest of the information from the school records. Else, just pass it on," the teacher said smiling, and left the class, giving the forms to Shreya Sharma, the girl sitting on the first seat. Smiling to herself, she left an excited class XI-A all abuzz about the competition.

"You'll take part, na?" Aanya asked, turning to me after spending a good time dreaming about the dance school with Aarav and herself in it. Oh, by the way, I forgot to mention that I am a dancer. Even though no one knows it except for Aanya and Aarav (credit to her that he knows, after which he laughed at me in my face, and left me so embarrassed)... I love dance, but I am super shy. Therefore, you have probably understood why no one else knows that I am a dancer.

"What? Me? Competition? Couple Dance? Are you sane?" I asked her.

She tilted her head to one side as she pouted cutely and said, "Yes. You. In an "International" couple dance competition. And yes, as a matter of fact, I am sane." Her extremely weird sense of humor surfaces so abruptly sometimes that I choose to ignore it without even laughing at her. She seemed to have noticed it, and raised an eyebrow.

"Listen Aanya, I would've but th..." Aarav who came to my seat interrupted me, "Aanya come back to our seat. We need to discuss about the dance competition. I am sure he does not know a word about the type of dance that I do. In fact, he never ever can." He said as he held her wrist and pulled her up. "But Aa..." she said but was interrupted by me as I held her other hand and shook my head from side to side to stop her from putting up a fight with Aarav for my sake.

In the past too, there had been a good number of fights between Aanya and Aarav because she always backs me and he always insults me. It is true that I have always loved Aanya, but I never like them fighting because then she is sad for the whole day and that bugs me so much. I love her but I do not expect anything at all in return from her. I am not that selfish as to put up a fight between her and the one she loves in order to make her mine. I have loved her the most and I cannot push her into hell just to decorate my heaven.

She turned towards me and sighed, giving up; I blinked my eyes reassuringly in reply. She shook her head from one side to the other, picked up her things and went off with him. The form was passed down to me, I looked at it and thought of what she had said, but passed it on to the people sitting behind me who were busy copying out assignments.

A few minutes later I turned back to see Aanya and Aarav filling up their names in the form. I sighed, imagining Aanya dancing and winning the competition with me, and then I shook off these thoughts knowing that such a thing would not be possible, and fished out a novel from my bag, "Is It Too Much To Ask For Love?" by Ariba Tahir. She is truly a great author.

The bell rang again shrilly, causing my ears to bleed, and Mrs. Simantika Kapoor came in to collect the forms. "All done?" she asked, earning affirmative nods from the students. "Okay give it to me," she said and took the form from Adiba Malik.

Adiba is a beautiful yet rebellious, most foul-mouthed but fun to be with, girl in our batch. She is beautiful and a good friend to be with, but is a total rebel and a little too caustic in speech for a geek like me to digest. Aanya even tried to hook Adiba up with me when we were in ninth standard, but things could not work out between us poles-apart people. If I am day, she is night, and if I am an old book, she is a laptop, and if I am sugar, she is nothing but smoking hot chili.

Adiba turned to me and noticed me looking at her, "Hey geek of the week... I mean Yuvraj! Vas Happenin?" she asked in a fake British accent, same as her idol whom she shares her surname with, Zayn Malik, from One Direction. I sighed at her and turned to ma'am without answering her. Bestowing on me an eye roll and a scowl, she sat down cursing.

Ma'am read the names to herself silently and continued, "I'll take up the names now, and if anyone else wants to take part, you may go to Mrs. Navneet Zandu, the office head." She paused as she pushed a strand of hair behind her ear, "Aisha Mishra and Ronit Sharma, Aanya Saeed and Aarav Singh and Shreya Sharma and Rajat Kashyap." She read out the names of the participant couples.

"You are not filling up, Yuvraj?" she asked me looking down at the form. "No partner ma'am," I sighed and looked down. She shook her head with understanding. "Please don't yell like wild jungle animals until sir comes. I'll be in a lot of trouble if you do," She announced as she looked up at the others and went off to her other class.

I checked the timetable... Economics. I did a little dance in my head whilst the others groaned; the semester marks were to be announced today. I had studied days and nights for the semester exams and was very eager to know how I had fared, while the others prayed to their stars to be sweet to them.

I saw Aanya and Aarav leaving the class with four other kids. "Aanya!" I called her; she turned back, "Bolo." "Where to?" I asked back pointing towards the door. She came to my seat and rested her hands over the table while whispering in my ears, "Test marks are to be announced...and competition is announced. So we are going for practice," she said in an 'I am so smart yet innocent' tone.

I rolled my eyes at her, "Achcha? Ms. Aanya Saeed's idea, right?" I said in a fake, 'you are such greatness' tone. She knew me a little too well not to understand from my tone that I was mocking her and not serious. She nodded, a frown covering her beautiful face.

I gave her a disgusted look and continued, "I guess you have forgotten that Mr. Arunab Desaai declares in the class the marks of those students also who are absent or out of class. Moreover, going out does not alter the fact that marks are to be announced and that Aarav sucks in Economics."

As I told her this, her expression grew tense. Thinking for some time, she said, "Ditch It! We will see what happened. Check my marks and tell me. Chalo bye. Okay?"

I rolled my eyes but agreed, "Okay!"

She opened her mouth; I knew what she was about to say. "Aanya, I swear I will throw you out of the window or into the dustbin if you speak in a "The fault in our stars" dialogue," I warned her.

She giggled cutely. "Perhaps, okay will be our always," she said in an Augustus Waters accent and ran off.

"I wish it were," I mumbled to myself.

"Morning, class!" Mr. Desaai entered, breaking my chain of beautiful thoughts.

He started calling out the marks after giving us a few minutes to settle down. After announcing the marks of all the numbers before twelve he called, "Roll number 12, Aarav Singh," making a disgusted expression at the same time.

"He has gone for dance practice, sir."

He nodded and continued, "14 on 40. Failed with extremely horrible marks." He shook his head and continued reading out the marks as I wrote down Aarav's marks, even though he had not asked me to.

A minute or two later, after arguing with Adiba over a mark that she had cheated to get, he called out, "Roll number 15, Aanya Saeed," and looked up.

"Sir, she too has gone for the dance practice."

He nodded and smiled at me; all of the school knew that both of us were very close and were best friends.

"38 on 40. Pass with very good marks."

I widened my eyes; Aanya scoring so well in Economics was a little shock to me, though I was of course very happy for her. Shaking off the thought and surprise, I did a little dance in my head and jotted down her marks.

A while later he was just three numbers away from my roll number. My heart ran at its fastest rate. I was so scared and tensed that I sent up prayers to all the 33 crore Gods and Goddesses of the Hindu religion and all the ten Sikh Gurus to bless me and make me score well. Even though I had full faith in myself as I had studied very hard, and knew that I had done well in the examination, still, you never know – anything can happen when it comes to test marks.

"The last student, roll number 48, Yuvraj Thakur Singh," he looked up at the class. My heart pounded ever so fast as if it would just tear through my chest and jump out. "... Has scored the maximum marks in the entire batch! 39.5 on 40 that rounds off as 40 on 40!" he said proudly as he handed me my paper and the entire class clapped for me. I felt elated and on top of the world. I was so proud and happy for myself that my hard work had really paid off. I happily thanked my stars, and all the 33 crore Gods, Goddesses and Sikh Gurus whom I had bothered with my pleas a little while ago.

He continued, "17 students out of the class of 48 have failed. Even though you were to score only 20 marks to pass..." He had an extremely disgusted expression on his face. "The top three students in the class are...third is Aanya Saeed with 38 marks," he smiled at me as the class rose up in applause. "Second is Ishaan Khattar with 39 marks, and the first position in the entire batch is bagged by Yuvraj Thakur Singh with full marks." He smiled at me as the entire class broke into loud applause.

Without another word he turned to the black board and started teaching "Growth, Information and Other Issues", a new chapter. I groaned, as I knew what was going to happen. I had to make notes for Aanya now. I almost wanted to bang my head against the wall or the blackboard, as I had to do double the work now. I sighed as I opened my book and acted as if I was deeply engrossed in the stupid and easy chapter, that I had already studied thoroughly the night before. It entails so much pain to have a lazy and naughty best friend who you can never say "No" to; you have to experience having such a friend to know my pain. However, you never will, because she is an only one of a kind.

2

I was sitting in the canteen, making notes for Aanya, which was ruining my lovely meal of burger and coke. Suddenly, someone tapped on my shoulder hard. I turned around. “Yuvraj dude, where are you? I have been looking for you ever since the world came into existence!” Aanya said in her usual habit of exaggeration, as she panted due to running or maybe due to her dance practice. “Were you or I even born in this body when the world came into existence?” I asked.

She opened her mouth to say something while thinking with narrowed eyes. “No. But... Whatever.” She rolled her eyes.

“Aanya! Are you like back from cutting rocks at a field or something? Look at you, you are exhausted. Take some rest and a few breaths, dude, it seems like you will die on your feet if you stand for a few more minutes!” I half pleaded and half ordered her.

“Don’t change the topic, Yuvraj Thakur Singh,” she warned me while wiping off the sweat, drinking my coke and earning an expression of disgust from me.

"By the way love, you owe me a party," I stated.

"What do you even mean" expression covered her face.

"You have scored 38 on 40," I gave her a cheeky grin as she widened her eyes.

"38 on 40! Really? And my rank?" she asked with crossed fingers.

"Third," I told her happily.

"Haww! Really? Third? Yaaaay!" she did a little dance that was not little at all as she was pouting and twirling her arms like a little kid in the air. "And you?" she asked quickly with narrowed eyes.

"First… 40 on 40," I said quietly.

"What is this dude? How on Earth can you bring full marks in Economics! Ever heard about limits? You cross them, you cross limits of perfection," she said in a fake 'this is too much' tone, but I knew she was happy.

"How much did Aarav score? Even though I know it won't be less than 25…," she asked causing bomb blasts to take place in the hollow of my stomach.

"Sit down first," I told her. She sat down next to me. "14 on 40…failed!" I exclaimed.

Aanya had a proud face but received this piece of information with an extremely betrayed expression as I cracked up.

"But he cheated for 25 marks worth of answering! How can he score 14?" she had a surprised expression covering her entire face.

"Karma is a bitch, baby!" I said and laughed again.

She raised her eyebrows, "Plch! Okay, ditch it. I want a favor," she changed the topic; I stopped her midway and made her drink water, "Now speak".

She started, "You already know that there is that Dance Championship that Mrs. Simantika Kapoor told us about in class, which I and Aarav have been practicing for," she said with pleading eyes.

"So?" I asked her.

"So I missed my Economics class today and... You know I H.A.T.E. Economics and I scored only because it was a chapter you explained to me four times in one week. So..." she told me and stopped for me to understand the rest.

"So Ms. Aanya Saeed wants me to make notes for the class?" I completed her sentence; she nodded sheepishly.

"Aanya dude!" I whined, "Please attend your classes, it takes loads and loads of time, effort and energy to do so much of work. My hands are aching," I said as I handed her the notes I had been making. "After that you drink my coke too," I chuckled.

She stared at me and ignored my comment. She returned to her usual chirpy self and squealed happily, as she hugged me, "You are the best! Thank You so fucking much Yuvraj. What would I do without you? I wonder!" Without even giving me a chance to hug back, she pulled away, looking at her notes.

"So I am not making notes for you again, I am tired," I warned her.

She puckered out her lower lip like a kid, "Then what is the use of having a topper best friend with exceptionally beautiful handwriting, sweetheart?" she teased me, still having the same face on.

"Friends with benefits quote are being taken too seriously here, huh?" Aarav's voice boomed, killing Aanya's pout as she instantly stood up.

"Ah Aarav!" He hugged her tightly causing explosions of jealousy inside me. "Hi baby," he greeted her. She gave him a totally fake smile that I alone could make out was fake.

I do not understand why Aanya does not stop him from calling her "baby", "babe", "bachcha" and what not stupid names, when she does not like being called by such names, as she told me. She suddenly grows up in front of Aarav; otherwise, she is always a cute, little kid around me.

Love is not growing up in front of your other half; it is being the little, naughty child that you really are, and not pretending or faking to be a grown up, serious and mature adult just to impress your loved one. It is not creating a fake image in the brain of the other person just to make yourself look good; that is not love, it is just attraction. Love is Love - it cannot be replaced by attraction or cooperation. Aanya is attracted to him and is also the only one cooperating, I can see that and maybe she too can, but has a fear somewhere inside her heart of losing him.

"Let's go, we're getting late for practice," he said to her, while pulling her up without even acknowledging me once. I furrowed my eyebrows, which she noticed, "At least say hi to Yuvi," she whispered to him in a low tone so that I would not hear it, but I heard it nevertheless.

"Firstly don't call him Yuvi, I don't like it when you do so," he said, causing Aanya's eyebrows to furrow this time. He continued, "Secondly, you know I do not like him. In fact, I hate him. How are you even friends with him, huh? I cannot even stand his sight, let alone being best friends. He is such a geek! Blah, he cannot even talk without being shy," he said quite loudly.

Ouch, that hurt hard. It felt as if someone had hit me hard in the ass or on the point where if hit hard in reality one can hit high notes in all songs with total perfection. If you know what I mean...

"Well, you have failed in Economics with an amazing score of 14 marks, where he and I have secured first and third positions. He scored full and I scored 38. He is attending all the classes and is the ideal student, whereas you are bunking classes just so that the teachers do not scold you for scoring awfully in semester exams. And, he is an idiot? Well, I do not think so. Actually, I think sensibly and my sense thinks the other way around," she defended me while making a round with her index finger gesturing 'other way around'.

I bit my lip awkwardly and looked down at my burger. "Anyways, I am not going," Aanya said to him in a stern tone, and sat down again.

"But why?" he asked her.

"Because I want to sit here, with Yuvi and I am not in the mood for a practice," she said casually, putting emphasis on my nickname in her typical 'I will do what I want' attitude that nobody except me can question, not even Aarav the great.

"What do you mean you are not in the mood?" he gasped. "Means that I will not practice right now. Need further elaboration?" she said sarcastically.

"Fine. Do what you want!" he said in an irritated tone, "That is what I am doing, love!" she said in her typical tone.

Unable to digest the embarrassment and insult from Aanya in my presence, he left off in a huff as quickly as possible without another word.

"You should not have fought with him for me, Aanya!" I told her.

"Oh Mr. Sweet Soul," she taunted me. "Okay fine he is my boyfriend and everything but this does not change the fact, and never will that you are my best friend. Moreover, Aanya Saeed has not given the right to anyone on Earth to hurt someone she is deeply attached to. Therefore, what he got was what he deserved. Get it?" she asked in an imperious tone, pointing her finger at me. As I could sense her temper rising, I nodded in agreement. "Good boy," she smiled, "I got to go for practice, bye." She got up and sipped from my cold drink again, "Thanks for the notes! You know I love you!" she yelled as she ran away giggling.

"I wish you were not saying that in jest," I mumbled and sighed.

I still remember the first day I saw her, four years back, when we were in VIIth standard. I was a typical, scared, tensed and raw new kid at St. Laurens' Academy, and she, being the attitude queen that she is, was the only girl no guy would dare to mess with in this life.

Flashback four years back

"Excuse me? Where is class VII A?" I asked a group of boys standing in the corridor.

"Who the fuck are you?" a boy asked me rudely.

"I am Yuvraj Thakur Singh, new student. Please stop abusing me and tell me where is VIIth A?" I asked him again.

"Okay, so you are a new student? You want to know the directions to go to your class? I shall tell you surely. But first dance for us, give us some entertainment!" he commanded.

I gave him a confused look.

"First dance for me then I will tell you where class VII A is, you motherfucking deaf boy!" he barked in my face. "Please do not use foul words when speaking of my mother. And, I am sorry to bother you but... I shall ask someone else," I said and tried to escape. Suddenly, I felt a hand on my collar pulling me from behind.

"Oh hero! I am Jai Dhingra, your senior. It will be good for you if you do not try to act smart yeah! I am the don of St. Laurens' Academy. Do what we say or it will land you up in very bad consequences," he said in a fake accent. He raised his hand to slap me and I closed my eyes tightly.

"Ae Jai! Kya? Problem kya hai teri huh?" A shrill voice was heard yelling from behind us. The boy, Jai Dhingra, stopped and looked behind me. A tall and beautiful girl in uniform and braided hair came up to us and jerked his hand away. "What happened?" she asked me.

"This..."

Jai interrupted me. "Aanya you please stay away from my matters!" he said to her. She stared at him from top to bottom, raised her eyebrows in a 'Think I will listen to you' expression, and ignored him.

"You speak up. What are they doing?" She asked me with a kind smile.

"This senior, Jai Dhingra, was standing here with all these boys and I came in and asked him the direction to class VII A. Out of nowhere, he said dance for me first and abused me with all those f words. I said no, I would ask the directions from someone else. So he threatened me saying that he was the don of the entire school and would have beaten me up if you had not made it here on time," I told her.

She listened carefully and I think I saw her jaw tightening. She turned to him, "Ae Jai Dhingre!" she said gesturing a drum purposely to piss him off. "You are a senior? Oh really? Since when? I guess you are of VII A only. Oh damn, I am sorry I forgot that you are a failure and had failed last year and the year before that, or else you would have been in ninth standard. You are the school don! Nice joke huh. Now, stop ragging students or I'll complain to Sister Elena and you'll be thrown out of school." As she threatened him, he was about to say something but she stepped forward as if backing him off. He pointed a finger at her and went off with his gang.

"Thank you so much for helping me out. I owe everything to you," I thanked her quickly.

"It's all right, relax! Oh, by the way I am Aanya Saeed. Your classmate… And that son of a bitch that just went by is also in our class," she smiled cutely as she said this, extending her hand to me.

I nodded and shook hands with her, "I am Yuvraj Thakur Singh. New Student. From St. Tessa Academy."

She nodded, "Come, let's go, otherwise we'll get late for class." Smiling she started walking and I quickly followed her.

I looked around the class, only one seat was empty, the last seat. I was going to sit there, as I did not want Aanya to pity me and make me sit with her.

"Hey Yuvraj! Where?" she asked me.

I pointed to the last seat.

"You are not going to sit alone on the last seat, are you?" she asked me.

I nodded.

"No you are not! Come and sit with me until you make some friends. After that you can go and sit with them." She pointed towards her seat and shrugged as if she did not mind sharing seats with me. I smiled at her warmly and thankfully and sat down with her.

Aanya thus became my partner for the entire year. It did not take us much time to jell, and soon we became best friends, as according to her I was different from the other boys at school. This clearly meant that I was innocent and did not use swear words in every second line of conversation. Her charm and simplicity made me fall hard for her within a few months. Call it childhood innocence or friendship or attraction, I loved her for who she is. What a girl!

End of flashback

I smiled to myself thinking of everything. I sighed and casually looked up at the watch; ten o' clock it said. Ten? Ten? Ten! Holy shit! I was late for my secret dance rehearsals. 10 am was the only time in the entire day when the rehearsal hall was empty. I packed up my things and ran off to the rehearsal hall.

3

Aanya

"five…four…three… Aanya!" Aarav said in an irritated tone.

"Sorry!" I apologized and tried again.

"… What the hell are you doing!? Where is your mind?" he yelled at me. "I-I'm sorry. I am just not able to dance today… I don't know why! Maybe I miss mom." I sighed, referring to my mom who passed away when I was three.

"I don't give a shit about it Aanya. Do it properly or back out early with your dancer best friend!" he said in a rude tone.

"Hey Aarav, why are you scolding me like this? And, if you have to take out historical grudges, then sit and do it okay. I said I am trying!" I said in a totally pissed off tone.

"You sit, keep trying and hang out with your friend. Yeah! I am going now! Go to hell!" he yelled and barged out of the rehearsal hall, not even caring to shut off the music system that had Saaware from Phantom blaring out of its speakers.

I was just not able to dance properly that day, repeated mistakes were happening, my mind was in a totally different world. I got so hurt by his words that my knees failed as tears flooded my eyes.

"Aanya! What's wrong?" I heard a voice from the other end of the room, and my mind registered that it was Yuvraj's. No, I cannot tell him, he will get upset just like that. "Nothing, w-what happened? I am good," I said, wiping away my tears quickly with the back of my hand.

"Stop lying! I've seen and heard every freaking thing that ass said," he said in a stern voice as his fists balled up.

"It's not his fault, Yuvi. I-I am not able to dance today. I deserved to get a scolding and I got it. It's okay!" I quickly backed Aarav.

"Come on Aanya! He was taking revenge because you backed me in the canteen. Moreover, he can't talk to you like this!" he complained.

I sighed. "I am fine with it. You do your own thing. He talked to me, right? What is your problem?" I snapped back. A horrified expression covered his face. "Fine" he said in an 'I give up' tone and went off.

Oh God! First, I had made Aarav angry and now Yuvraj. Why couldn't I control my anger? I was already regretting my stupid deed of hurting him for no reason. Just because he tried to help me, I had snapped at him. Can't help, I was too angry to realize anything right then. Aarav was surprisingly very rude to me that day, and so I showered all my anger on Yuvraj. I was so pissed off, I could not dance, and everyone was trying to order me about or control me; I am not one to be ordered around. Sighing, I got up on to my feet, packed up my things, and went off home. I needed some rest for the sake of humanity, so that I do not kill anyone in my anger.

4

"Aarav!?" I gasped as I stared at him. He was dancing with Rakshita Jain, the girl who had a crush on him, and horror of horrors! - They were dancing to the same song we had been practicing on yesterday. "Oh! Aanya! Hi!" he said casually, as if nothing had happened yesterday or as if his dancing with Rakshita was not at all a big deal, whereas, I was still angry over his behavior the day before. "May I know why the hell you are dancing with her?" I crossed my arms on my chest.

"Because she wanted to learn the moves, and so did I," he said in his typical 'I wanted to, so I did' tone.

I gasped. "Just because she wanted to learn the moves, so you will dance with her to the same song that we were dancing on yesterday?" I said in a disbelieving tone. I was feeling as if my eyeballs were about to pop out of my eye sockets.

"I am a better dancer than you. Mind your own freaking business, Aanya Saeed!" The nosy-posy Rakshita interfered in between.

"You are better than me?" I asked her.

She nodded in her arrogant, bitchy way. At first, I laughed mockingly and then continued, "Then I guess there should be a faceoff. C'mon, let's see who is better than whom!" I challenged her in full confidence.

She nodded and pouted as she checked me out; I gestured to Aarav to make space for us to dance, which he quickly did.

I loosened my shirt and tied my hair and my ghungroos. "Let's face it girl!" I said as I played Payaliya from DevD on the music system.

"Don't you tell me! Bharatanatyam, like really?" she said in a fake accent, as if she were the queen of Belgium and Indian dance styles were useless and very silly.

"Oh My God! I am 'really' telling you. Bharatanatyam is the dance you have to do! Dancers can sculpture themselves into any dance," I smirked at her.

"Huh fine!" she replied in a huff.

Aarav stared at me as I tried to ignore him. I felt very anxious, angry and miserable; I just wanted to cry as the stare of his deep, black eyes burned under my skin. At last, ignoring the tension and anger engulfing me, I took my place and waited for the soft flow of music to begin. Once it started, I took a step forward and did the namashkar that is done before any performance. As the song progressed, I felt relaxed, and allowed a small smile to form on my lips. I turned elegantly, my body in tune with the slow music, my postures and mudras falling in place beautifully. My arms moved effortlessly, flowed and fell in place all on their own, my legs were as if they knew which beat wanted them to do which jump or tap. My expressions synchronized blissfully, and described perfectly what the girl was telling, all about how her 'piya' is and how her anklet or 'payaliya' wants her to go to her piya's house.

Yet, there was a sort of harshness to me, as if I were someone who should not be underestimated. I did not quite care at that point of time. My heartbeat was growing steadily along with it. Dance is what just temporarily disconnects me from the miseries all around, and transports me into my own little dreamland. Dance has made me who I am today and doing it seems more natural to me than my own heartbeat. Dance was the thing I can truly say I was born with; I have grown up dancing. My performance was perfect I guess; everything from my breathing to how my feet moved stayed in perfect sync. All my thaaps, postures, mudras and expressions seemed totally interconnected, as if my body knew when to do what. The sound of my ghungroos was the most melodious sound for me; my ghungroos are one of the few things I worship.

If, by the end of this dance my breath were to be taken away, I would know the exact reason why, because I had put all my soul and heart into that moment. The tunes were soft but not subtle, clearly stating their intention of taking me along with them. That was when I decided to let go...let my sadness, my anger, and anxiety go...

Right here, right now, I was living. Nothing else seemed to matter anymore; I allowed the music to take me wherever it pleased on the dance floor. It sped up, I sped up. When the song ended I gracefully took up my final thaap and posture, I suddenly felt so complete.

Suddenly, I was broken from my trance of thoughts when Aarav's applause filled my ears. For those few minutes, I was taken off to a new world where I had forgotten the existence of Aarav and Rakshita. I could not help but smile proudly at the mirror as I stood in my aramandalam position. At that very moment, I wondered why I had not seen it before - dancing was the one and only thing for me. In my eyes, because of that dance, I could see how perfect it truly made me feel. I had done my level best today proving that nothing in the world could separate me from my dance.

I got up and did the final namashkar, took off my ghungroos and brought them up to my forehead. Dance has made me a spiritual person; it has made me realize that God truly exists. In the form of ghungroos, gurus and vandanas, I realized that God is there. I joined my hands and thanked God for blessing me with this divine talent.

"That was so damn Indian! Now I will show you real dance!" Rakshita said in a bitchy way. As I played the same song for her, she started sitting in a way in which people sit and shit. Later she made some nonexistent mudras. I have never ever ever seen such a horrible Bharatanatyam dance performance, like...ever. No mudras, postures, thaaps or expressions matched with the tune of the song or even fell together. Her ghungroos made negligible sound.

She slipped midway trying to do an allarippu step and started crying as I laughed my head off even though I was taught never to laugh when anyone trips.

"Poor kid! Someone said she is a better 'dancer' than I am. But what I can see is that you are not even a dancer; leave alone better than me love!" I said as I rolled my eyes at her.

"Babe you were too good!" Aarav flew to my side. I winced at 'babe', it sounds very cheesy and pathetic to call someone babe; yet, I did not say a word.

"Nope!" I said popping the 'p', "I'm not! She is, yeah?" I gave him a disgusted expression as I started walking out of the room; I just hated him for talking to me rudely and then being bipolar. "Oh, and as a matter of fact, I will not be doing practice for the next two days; I have to go to Delhi for my cousin's wedding." I said that casually as I straightened my shirt, opened my hair and packed my ghungroos. I laughed as I saw in the mirror, Rakshita still crying on the floor.

"Two days, baby!?" he gasped and I groaned inside at the nickname for the zillionth time.

"Yes two days." I replied.

"Why so?" he asked with a lot attitude.

"Well, be thankful that I told you once, but regret that you did not hear it. Secondly, I am not answerable to you," I shrugged as I started walking off. "Oh, and enjoy with the butterflies swooning over you, because, guess what? I don't give a living shit!" I rolled my eyes and left him in confusion and shock even though I hated myself for doing that.

"Yuviii!!" I yelled as I saw a tall figure walking ahead, with black, square framed glasses and curly hair. He turned back with a frown, blinked once as he saw me, turned again and started walking off. Oh, damn! He is upset due to my behavior yesterday. I sighed as I ran at my full speed, "Yuvraj dude I am sorry! I am so fucking stupid to yell at you for no fucking reason in the world. Sorry na! I was very very very pissed off, and you know how short tempered I am." I pleaded, as I gradually realized that I was using 'fucking' a bit too many times.

"Short tempered? Pissed off? At Aarav? Then why did you send me off so rudely?" he asked as his eyebrows furrowed together developing a cute frown on his face.

"Arre! You barged in suddenly and I saw you just after being yelled at so I...you know...kind of...got upset!"

I bit my lip, and he sighed. "Last time!" he warned me.

"Thank Youu!!" I hugged him as he chuckled. "Listen, please please copy all the work for two days. It is Tanya di's wedding at Delhi and I'm going tomorrow," I said, giving him a cheeky-requesting grin and batting my eyelashes.

He sighed, "Ahhan! Fine. But come back soon." He looked sad.

"Aww! You will miss me?" I asked him in a kidding manner. "Of course I will. What will I do here without you," he said seriously.

I looked him in the eyes as a flash of truth passed through them. I nearly drowned in his green, beautiful eyes when I realized he was Yuvraj not Aarav.

"You are my one and only friend after all," he looked down as he continued. I nodded.

"Now I got to go do packing! I will meet you later! Bye!" I cooed as he rolled his eyes and waved me goodbye.

5

"Rajdhani Express is on platform number three. Passengers are requested to kindly take their respective seats."

An announcement was made as I stood on the platform with my dad. I had brought my earphones to listen to songs but I was just sitting on my suitcase, staring at the railway tracks. I was feeling just very weird and scared, as if I was about to miss some train; a vague anxiety, the cause of which I could not identify. I didn't know, I just felt very low.

"Aanya come!" dad shook my shoulders breaking my chain of thoughts.

"Yeah dad I'm here," I smiled a little and followed him into the train.

I went in, counted seats and sat down at the window seat. I fished out my phone from my pocket - two new messages from two new conversations, the screen flashed. I entered the password (which was Yuv And Aan, so that Aarav could not make it out however much he tried). One message from Aarav, 'Will you not practice today?' - So he had clearly forgotten that I was heading for Delhi; this was quite expected of him. I sighed, thought of clearing his doubt, and decided against it.

One message from Yuvraj, "Have mauj Aan. Will miss you and will surely take care of that ass...oops I mean Aarav : P. Bye. Happy Journey! Xx." I laughed at the message. "Achcha Yuvraj daddy : P. Take care of that ass xD. Bye, will miss you too. Xx," I replied and laughed at our tuning and stupidity.

I looked up and was a bit shocked to see that I was so engrossed in my thoughts regarding Aarav and Yuvraj that I had not even realized, ditch it, I did not even feel once that the train had started moving. Spreading and crossing my legs while I tried to ignore my weird feeling, I settled down to listen to music by connecting my earphones with my phone playing They Don't Know About Us from Take Me Home by One Direction as it was the first song in my playlist.

A few hours later, when the train stopped at a station, I pulled out my earphones that were playing 'Little Things' from 'Take Me Home' by One Direction. I got down from the train to buy a few books that were required for the journey, as I knew that I would get bored during the long journey. As I got in, the train started moving, and I stood at the door and opened my hair, enjoying the beautiful, cold breeze hitting my face and making my hair fly all over my face.

I wish I had known then that I would soon regret my decision to stand at the door instead of going in to be with my dad. I would never have got down even from the train, let alone stand at the door.

6

Yuvraj

"Where is she!? Damn, this girl!" I heard Aarav yell while he walked back and forth in the corridor, occasionally moving his hands through his hair in stress. He turned to where I was standing and spotted me.

"Hey you, Yuvraj! Where the hell is your best friend forever? She is not replying to my messages even once!" he asked me in a disgusted tone.

"In the train," I told him.

"Train? Why on Earth is she on a train?" he asked in a shocked way.

"She is travelling," I told him yet again, testing his patience.

He made a face, "Wow! Thank you for the enlightenment, brother! Travelling where, you fool?"

I rolled my eyes, "Speak that way na! She's travelling to Delhi," I said in a 'you should know that much at least' tone. My reply took him by surprise.

"Delhi? Why is she going to Delhi?" he asked me.

"Um, she might not have told you, but it is Tanya di's," (he raised his eyebrows at the mention of Tanya di) I sighed, "Her cousin's wedding; so she will be there for two days," I informed him.

"Heavens! Yes! She had told me. I thought she was joking... Hell!" he started cursing and swearing.

Suddenly his phone rang. "Where are you Aanya baby?" he cooed as he picked up the call. He frowned a bit, "Um, sorry who is this?" he asked. "Yes I am Aanya's boyfriend. What happened?" he asked again, a stunned expression hitting his face.

I shook him. "What happened?" I mouthed, as I grew tense.

"Shut the fuck up right now," he mouthed back as he nodded to the other person. "Oh my God, sir! I will be there, sir; you please take her to the hospital," he exclaimed in extreme anxiety. Disconnecting the call, he started to go away.

"Hey hey Aarav! What happened to Aanya? Why in the world will they take her to the hospital? Where are you going?" I shot questions at him all in one breath as I gripped his muscular hand.

"Aanya fell down from the train, she is in Holy Family Hospital... I am going there straight away. Her condition is not good; she is in the operation theatre." Saying this, he went off without explaining anything further to me.

I just could not believe what I had heard...why was Aanya in the hospital? How did she fall down from the train? I ran down at my fastest speed to the parking lot and hopped into my car, driving at a break-neck speed. I did not care if I got a speeding ticket, Aanya and her conditions were more important to me than 1000 bucks. My stomach twisted at all the possibilities running through my mind. "Please say she is okay, please," my mind yelled as tears formed in my eyes. I found my way quickly and parked my car in the parking lot. Aarav had already made it to the hospital as I could see from his bike parked next to me.

7

I wiped off my tears and entered the lobby of the hospital.

"Aanya," I took a deep breath, "Aanya Saeed?" I asked the receptionist as I banged my palm on her table.

She seemed to be shocked at my sudden demand but typed something on the computer in front of her. "Aanya Saeed. Fourth floor, emergency ward. However, visiting her is not permitted. A..." I ran towards the lift, not waiting for her to finish.

I pressed the buttons furiously. "Come on you fool!" I yelled, smacking the damn thing. Not waiting any more, I rushed towards the stairs.

Four flights of steps later, I was breathing and panting heavily, my hands clutched to my sides as I landed myself on the fourth floor. As I looked around the room numbers, I bumped into someone... Aarav. He looked dazed.

"How is she?" I asked him. Instead of replying, he gulped hard, tapped my shoulder lightly, shook his head from side to side and went past me.

I was pretty confused at the reaction I received. He would react that way only if something horrible had happened to her, and it looked as though he was going to leave her all alone in the hospital.

Out of nowhere, my phone buzzed. "Hello?" I received the call.

"Is it Yuvraj there?" a male voice spoke on the other side.

"Yes. Who is it?" I questioned.

"I am Omair Saeed, Aanya's father... How is my daughter?" he said in a heavy voice.

"Um, I do not know sir. I have just reached the hospital. Can I talk to the doctor, check on her, and then tell you?" I asked him.

I could hear him sob. "Okay son. Thank you." he said...

I could hear him sob at the other end. "Beta," he said, "I came to know that she had been pushed down only after the train had left. The Railways contacted me asking me to get down at the next station and rush back. They were taking her to hospital immediately, without waiting for me. I did get down and was coming back by taxi, when I got a call from Delhi saying that my mother had suffered a heart attack and is critical. I called the hospital where Aanya was being taken, and the doctors assured me that they would take all due care. I shall come back as soon as my mother is slightly better. Son, I am depending on you to take care of her in my absence."

"Sure, Uncle. I shall be with her throughout, don't worry," I assured him.

"Thank you so much, Beta," he said, disconnecting the call.

My parents had gone on a pilgrimage, leaving me at home, as I could not afford to miss classes. I decided that I would remain at the hospital as a bystander, instead of going home.

As I disconnected the call, the doctor came out. "How is Aanya?" I asked him quickly.

"Didn't Mr. Aarav tell you anything?" he asked in surprise.

"No sir, what is wrong?" I asked, my impatience getting the worst of me.

"She was thrown down from a moving train by two men, she... I am sorry but..." he stopped.

"But what!?" I yelled.

"But she has lost a leg. Her right leg was cut when she came under the train. It is a mercy that she did not suffer more severe injuries. We have to amputate the leg below the knee, but we are waiting till she stabilizes a bit, as she has lost a lot of blood, and is under shock." He stared at his shoes as he sighed heavily.

"W-what? She will not be able to w-walk?" I asked him in agitation.

"She will be. But she has to wait some time for that. Once we fix a prosthetic leg she will be able to walk, but as I told Mr. Singh when he asked...she will not be able to dance." He sighed and left me to my shock and anguish.

Hang on! Aarav had asked him if she could dance. Shit, how selfish could he be! I sighed at the thought of what I would say to Aanya if she were to ask about Aarav.

I called out to the doctor. "Sir, can I meet her?" I asked him.

He nodded to indicate 'no'. "At this hour?" he widened his eye. I checked the clock, 5:00pm, and hospital visiting hours were until 4:00pm.

"Please sir…just once," I requested him. He stared at me for some time and maybe sensing my dedication or maybe due to my height, he sighed heavily.

"You are her boyfriend?" he asked me.

"No sir, best friend," I admitted. He nodded and led me down the hallway and into a small room.

I stepped inside, he pulled back the curtain, and I saw her. And I lost my breath. She was lying there in a white, loose gown, her hair all scattered above her head, paler than I had ever seen, with dark blue circles under her eyes. Her veins were much more prominent than they usually were, and hooked up to her were about a million machines, wires and tubes. Her hands had about no skin visible due to the wires and tubes connected to them. Her mouth was slightly open; a transparent tube was pushed down through it, which carried food to her mouth while she was unconscious, I guess.

That was not where Aanya belonged. That was not how she ever in this life deserved to be. She deserved happiness and dance, not pain and a prosthetic leg.

Numb from what I was seeing, I stood completely still. How much I wanted to pick her up and hug her ever so tight! But she looked so fragile that I feared she would shatter and collapse then and there on the floor if I were to do so.

Eventually, I managed to get my feet to shuffle towards the bed; never had I looked at a bed with as much horror and anger as I was looking at that one. Up close she looked even worse, just so unlike her. She did not look asleep, she looked dead, and I could not stop myself from crying at the mere sight of her lying there lifeless.

"You have just one hour," the doctor sighed and left me with Aanya. I stroked her forehead gently and held one of her hands pierced with needles. "Aanya, hi, this is me. Yuvraj. How are you now?" I whispered in a low voice so that she could not hear. I turned away to the other side and cried. "Yuv-v-raj..." A thin voice hit my ears. "Aanya?" I swung back.

She had her eyelids opened with much difficulty, she looked as if she was high on weed but actually, she was high on medicines. She tried to get up. "Hey hang on! I got you," I said as I pushed a button on the side of her bed, which helped her sit straight. "Do you want to tell me something?" I asked her as I noticed she was fiddling her fingers and sweating. She nodded. "Go on," I gestured to her.

8

"I got down from the train one station after boarding, to buy a few books. As I got in, I saw that the weather was very pleasant with a nice wind blowing, so I stood at the door of the compartment to enjoy it. Little did I know that enjoying the weather would cost me so much." She started to cry, I rubbed her back, "C-cost? What ever happened Aanya? How did you fall? Did you lose your balance and fall down?" I shot questions at her.

"I was standing at the door; two boys came over and started harassing me. When I tried to push them away, one of them slapped me and tore the skirt I was wearing. Being the short-tempered person I am, I slapped him right across his face and said tons of colored words to him. He grew angry at the slap and…and…and the-they kicked me down like this," she tried to show me how they had kicked her. As she tried to move her leg, she cried out in pain because her leg had been cut while coming under the train, and only her thigh moved.

"I cannot feel my leg Yuvraj, my-my leg! Wh-what happened to me, Yuvi?" She asked me.

I stood up and shook my head, "Nothing happened to you Aanya." I lied to her. Being my best friend, she immediately spotted the lie.

"Don't you lie, Yuvraj Thakur Singh and tell me what happened!?" she yelled.

I remained quiet, as I could find no words to tell her that she had lost her leg and her dreams.

She pushed me a little away from the bed and pulled up the white sheet the nurse had covered her with; her expression was as if someone had betrayed her, left her all alone in a devastating situation. She saw it, her right leg, of which only the knee and thigh were left now. She was not able to understand what had happened, as if her brain had short-circuited and needed to be rebooted. She was all numb and motionless. How could this happen to her!

She stared at her leg for what seemed like forever, too weak and shocked to speak as realization hit her hard. She pressed the tips of her fingers into her eyes until she saw nothing but sparkles. She opened her mouth but it appeared as if she had choked, no words found their way out as she was bursting into tears.

Devastated with what she saw, she tried to lie down, but it was more like a stumble and fall that left her in a trembling heap on the bed. Tears were filling her eyes; I probably could hear her heart pounding at its fastest rate, as she was continuously rubbing her bandaged knee.

She looked up at me; I wanted so much to run away when I saw her expression, the always happy and chirpy Aanya was today weak, fragile and in tears. Her face was red from all the crying. Her eyes were venting out all the pain that she had in her heart through the salty water that was streaming down her cheeks; she was trembling and shaking. "My-my leg Yuvraj," she stammered in a hoarse voice.

"How did this h-happen?" She cried softly.

I just could not say anything.

"HOW DID THIS HAPPEN!?" She yelled in her loudest voice.

"When you were thrown from the train, then..." I stopped.

"Then what?" she yelled.

"Then your right leg came under the t-train and it got cu..." I stopped as I sighed for her to understand the rest.

"I will not be able to walk," she said to herself.

"No, no, you will be able to." I told her.

She looked up, "How?" A ray of hope crossed her eyes.

"They will fit you with a prosthetic leg after which you will be able to walk around..." I told her. She nodded. My voice was calm and strong despite my entire body being shaken on the inside. I masked my hurt, my pain, my weakness and put up a strong face so that I would have the courage and energy to handle her pain.

"And dance?" she asked in a 'hoping without hope' tone looking down and waiting for disappointment to hit her hard, and it did.

"No." People do not give much worth to two simple alphabets, but my speaking those two simple alphabets left her betrayed; the words rolled out of my mouth and she sat down there staring and crying softly at her leg, fate and situation.

"Did Aarav come here?" she asked me simply. Now was the big moment, I had to tell her that Aarav had deserted her on knowing the fact that she could not dance anymore. "Yuvraj bolo to dude!" she shook me, breaking my chain of thoughts. I sighed, "Um, he-he does not know. I will tell him as soon as I reach school." I looked down.

"Then where were you when you got to know about this?" she frowned a bit.

"At home. Like obviously, I do not live in a tent." I pretended to toss sarcasm at her.

"You skipped school!" she widened her eyes.

"Yeah had some assignment to do." I smiled a little at her; she nodded.

"Expected so." She murmured to herself so that I could not hear but I did.

There was a knock on the door. "Yes," I said.

"Sir, the doctor is calling you," the nurse said and smiled at me.

I nodded and turned back to Aanya, "I need to go check what he is saying. You rest and relax yeah?" I asked her. She nodded and gave me a little smile.

I went to the doctor. "Come in," he said as I knocked on the door.

"Sir, Patient ward number three. Aanya Saeed, I am her friend, Yuvraj Thakur Singh." I smiled at him; he nodded and gestured to me to sit down.

"Where is her boyfriend or her family? Don't they care about her?" he asked me.

"Her boyfriend probably doesn't care, as I saw him going away from the hospital when he came to know that she had suffered a disability. Her family members are unable to come as her grandmother has suffered a heart attack. Her father spoke to me requesting me to be with her till he is able to rush back." I replied.

"Her father has spoken to the hospital authorities, given consent for the various procedures, and sent money for the operation and the follow up procedures. We shall take the measurements of her leg tomorrow, so as to determine the size of the prosthesis, and the amputation will be carried out day after tomorrow. Thereafter, if all goes well, we can fit her with an interim prosthesis in a week to ten days time. This is to help her to get used to wearing a prosthesis, and to learn to walk with it. Once she is comfortable, we can discharge her from hospital. The permanent prosthesis can be fitted any time between two to six months after the amputation, according to the pace of her recovery and adjustment to it," he informed me. "Any queries, please come to me." He smiled and I nodded.

I left his room and went to her ward; she was sleeping peacefully under the influence of the sedatives the nurse had just given her. I went to her side and held her hand, and I sang in a low voice to her 'Jeepster' by T.Rex. I did not sleep a wink and kept holding her hand, occasionally stroking her head.

At 5:30am the sun shone bright and its light made Aanya's face glow like a million stars, the birds chirped and that very moment I realized that Musoorie looked breathtaking during sunrise, as breathtaking as every moment I had shared with the girl whom I loved the most and who had no idea about my feelings. Had I known this day would change things between us I would have been happy instead of being nostalgic.

9

At 8:00AM I had a sudden urge to pee; I let go of Aanya's hand slowly in order to keep her asleep and went to the washroom. As I came back to the room, I saw Aanya sitting up on the bed.

"Good Morning!" I wished her as I entered.

"Why did he go without meeting me?" she whined and asked like a kid.

I gave her a confused look.

"Aarav. Why did Aarav go without meeting me? I felt him holding my hand all night. He was here, right?" she asked me with bright eyes.

I could not say no and break her heart so I smiled, "Yes, he had come and he was with you. But, you know how school is and his attendance is already low, so he could not skip, and also you were sound asleep, so he went away without waking you up." I lied to her and gave her a fake smile; she nodded in an understanding way.

The nurse knocked and entered the room, "Good Morning, Aanya! How are you feeling?" she asked her.

"I am good, thank you," she said in response and the nurse smiled at her.

"I must say you are one very lucky girl to have a boyfriend like him. Such a sweet boy," she said. Aanya raised an eyebrow at me and I almost froze in my place.

"You do not know?" the nurse asked. She shook her head from side to side. "He was sitting with you here all night holding your hand, and he did not get any sleep and kept singing to you. He loves you a lot, my girl, never let him go." She smiled at me as I stared wide-eyed at Aanya. She appeared a bit surprised.

Aanya

The nurse's words processed in my brain on one side and Yuvraj's lie on the other; things started connecting in my brain. Aarav had not even visited me once and it was Yuvraj who had been sitting with me all night.

Realization hit me hard, Yuvraj had feelings for me, and Aarav did not give a shit about me. I sighed, "Thank you for telling me and making me realize this." I smiled at her, she returned it.

"Have your medicine, it is kept here." Taking up the tray in her hand, the nurse excused herself.

I looked up at Yuvraj with a questioning expression. "Um, n-no. Aarav was there. Really!" he lied.

"You know Yuvraj Thakur Singh, a few times it does happen that you lie and I do not catch you, but mostly I do, and this is one such time that I have caught you." I told him indirectly that I had realized everything, and he cast his looks down.

"Aarav never came, did he?" I asked him directly. He shook his head.

"Speak and answer my questions." I ordered him.

"No, he never came after the day of the accident." He spoke in a low voice.

"You were with me all night, now weren't you?" I asked again.

"Yes," he confessed.

"You were lying to me na?" I asked him again.

"Yes," he said, looking down.

"You have feelings for me no?" I asked him.

"Yes," he spoke up, but soon widened his eyes on realizing what he had said. "Ah, um, uh, No no. I-I..." he struggled to find an explanation.

"I know. It is good that at least someone loves me." I smiled genuinely at him, he faked a smile. "Since when, may I ask, and expect a true answer?" I crossed my arms.

"Seventh standard." He said in such a low voice that it sounded like a mumble. I stared wide eyed at him, "S-Seventh?" I asked to confirm. Looking up slowly he nodded.

It meant that ever since he had come to St. Laurens' he had loved me, and yet he had never told me or tried to cause a fight between Aarav and me. I sighed, "Aarav knows about my leg?" I asked him. "He does." He answered back as if he were at fault; he looked up and locked eyes with me.

His green eyes were as deep as an ocean, I wanted to just keep looking and drown in those beautiful eyes forever and ever. I had never felt as safe and secure in anybody's presence as I felt in his. I suddenly wanted to rewind time, fall for him back in seventh standard, and reject Aarav. Life would have been beautiful if I had had Yuvraj in the past and not him. I just so badly wanted to stand up on the top of a building and yell, "How could I not see him?" with bells ringing and wind blowing as they show in movies. I obviously did not feel that way, but I felt so special and so happy. Was I falling for him?

"Sir, Doctor Daanyaal Zaid is calling you," the nurse barged into the room breaking our eye contact and replacing the romantic air between us with an awkward one. "I'll g-go," he said quickly and went off.

10

Yuvraj

I left the room quickly smiling to myself. She knew about my feelings now, but I had a lurking fear in me that she would break our friendship. Thinking about the consequences, I went in to Doctor Daanyaal Zaid's cabin. "May I?" I asked him knocking at the door. "Sure," he replied and smiled at me.

"Did you send for me?" I asked him as I took a seat in front of him.

"Yes I did. We will take the measurements of Ms. Aanya Saeed today for the prosthetic leg, and then 3 days later the operation will take place," he informed me with a smile. I nodded. "Thank you for supporting her through all this, not many people do. She needs constant emotional support at this very difficult time, and in the absence of her parents, only a close friend can provide that to her." He said, patting my shoulder.

"She is my friend sir, I had to do it," I said and excused myself.

"We want one favor from you." He said, looking up as he called me.

"Yes sir," I asked him.

"Take this soup and make her drink it. She needs to recoup her strength fast." He told me with pleading eyes.

I sighed, "This is indeed a tough job to do." I sighed at him, and he gave me a helpless expression. Sympathizing with him, I agreed, "I will try my level best." I took the bowl from him and went to her ward.

As I was about to knock I heard Aanya cursing in a low tone. I went inside, and seeing her stare at her phone with all the anger in her eyes, "What is up with you Aanya?" I asked, startling her. "Uh, n-nothing," she lied.

"Stop lying Aanya," I told her. She handed me her Moto G with clenched jaws and balled fist, "I so hate him." She frowned.

I took her phone and saw a WhatsApp message from Aarav, "I am sorry Aanya, but we cannot let this be going on. You have lost a leg and will not be able to dance, while for me dancing is everything and I cannot spend my life with a physically impaired girl. Dance is what I live for; I am dating Noor and will perform with her in the competition. Sorry. Aarav xx."

I raised my eyebrows at it and winced, "He is such a son of a bitch," I murmured. "You are right!" she spoke up so vehemently that it took me by surprise.

"What?" I asked her.

"You are so right. He is a motherfucking son of a bitch! Bloody asshole! I-I pray that the stage on which he dances breaks, no no, a fire breaks out on it and - and Noor steps over him and - and he falls down and hurts his privates so hard that his future wives are not able to have children. Let me meet him, I am going to punch his dick ever so hard. I swear Yuvraj, kutte ki maut marega vo, keede padenge usko! Go to hell Aarav!" she was talking like a child and appeared very cute. Unable to stifle my laughter I giggled and she glared at me.

"What made you laugh like an elementary school girl?" she raised her eyebrows at me.

"You look so cute right now, just like Kareena Kapoor from Jab We Met. You even used her dialogue that 'Kutte ki maut marega' and 'Keede padenge' one." She broke into a smile, "You know how to make me smile, no?" she questioned chuckling, "You are my best friend for such reasons only," she laughed.

"Oh by the way your measurements will be taken today to get the correct size of the leg. You have to go through a small surgery after three days to clean up the portion below your knee, and to prepare it for getting the prosthesis fixed. You have to be very strong and brave, and you have to drink up this soup right now." I said presenting the bowl to her like some great chef offering a new and delicious dish. She frowned and pinched her nose up like a kid. "I do not want to drink it!"She whined. "Want or not want, you have to drink it like a good girl," I said, and made her drink it up even though she threatened that she would kill me after finishing it.

I was sent out of the room so that she could change, and I went down for a coffee.

11

"I hate you but I miss you," I heard her murmur to herself; I went inside and saw her staring at Aarav's Instagram pictures with Noor. "AANYA!" I tapped her shoulder, yelling playfully at the same time.

"Yuvraj! Are you a total gone case? You scared the living shit out of me! I will die someday due to this." She yelled, gasping with her hand pressed to her heart, dropping the phone in fright.

"Show me what you are looking at," I tried to snatch her phone but she took it and twisted her hand to the other side of her waist. I bent down and held her one hand while grabbing her other hand, in which she held her phone, without realizing that our faces were just inches apart. I felt her grip loosening on her phone, and looked up at her face feeling her breath hitting me on my face. She bit her lip while scanning my face while I gazed at her fascinated and got lost in her beauty.

Her phone buzzed, breaking our little, romantic moment. I quickly pulled back holding her phone in my hand. "Come on Aanya! You are seeing his photos!" I exclaimed.

She looked down, "Insta is in my phone... I came across them, so I..." she stopped midway.

"Block both of them, you will feel better. From Instagram, Facebook, WhatsApp, Twitter and all the social networking sites you use. Delete all his photos also. You will feel like Geet from 'Jab We Met'," I said giving her the phone.

"This is not 'Jab We Met', Yuvraj, and I am not Geet, he is not Anshuman and you are not...um, uh...what is the name... Shahid Kapoor!" she exclaimed.

"First things first, he was Aditya Kashyap and not Shahid Kapoor," I told her.

She raised her eyebrows at me. "But, the real name was Shahid Kapoor!" she stated.

"But, we are talking about 'Jab We Met', not real life. So... Aditya Kashyap not Shahid Kapoor!" I am a big JWM fan and no one can prove me wrong in it.

"Why did we drift away from the love triangle between you, me and Aarav to 'Jab We Met'?" She asked in an irritated tone.

"Love triangle?" I asked her.

"I love you and you both love me, isn't this a love triangle!?" she yelled with a straight face but widened her eyes on realizing what she had just said.

"You love me?" I asked her. She blinked her eyes multiple times and looked down as her cheeks became illuminated a deep shade of red.

"Don't tell me you are blushing?" I teased her. She smiled while looking down but looked up with a straight face, "You watch it!"She pointed her finger at me as I face palmed again because she tried to copy Hazel Grace Lancaster from TFIOS.

She laughed and blocked Noor and then Aarav from Facebook, Twitter, Instagram and Whatsapp. I could see relief flowing through her eyes as she deleted his number, pictures, message string, and WhatsApp chat and blacklisted his number.

"Come for taking the measurement," I said. She looked around in a helpless way and turned to me with sad eyes, unable to understand how to go.

"I got you," I said and lifted her up in bridal style. She looked at me, "I am heavy, am I not?" she asked innocently. I sighed and shook my head from side to side. "Very," I whispered in her ear and started laughing. She pinched up her nose. "Just kidding my love, just kidding," I said to her while landing her in the wheelchair.

"Thank you so much!" she chirped. We went off to Doctor Daanyaal Zaid's cabin, where I made her stand up on her one leg, with great difficulty, taking my support and propping her up against the wall. He took her measurements from her right knee till the ground. As soon as the doctor said, "Done, now you may sit down," she jumped on to her chair and took a deep breath. "It is so tough to stand," she said and went off to her ward.

12

3 days later

"What are you doing in your phone?" I asked Aanya as I got up from my slumber to see her tapping the screen of her phone.

"Writing random thoughts," she said, still tapping.

"Go to sleep, Aanya it is three in the morning," I told her.

"It is two fifty in the morning, not three, and I am not sleepy as yet," she said without even looking at me. I sighed, giving up and went off to sleep.

I woke up to some loud knocks and opened my eyes to see the nurse smiling at me.

"Morning." I mumbled to her.

"Good morning, sir. It is already seven in the morning; the operation will take place at four in the evening. Aanya is in the washroom." She told me and went off. I yawned and turned around to see Aanya coming out of the washroom.

"Morning Yuvi!" she chirped. As she came closer, I saw dark circles under her eyes.

"When did you finally sleep yesterday?" I asked her.

"Um, three thirty in the morning," she grinned.

"I can see that in...oops... I mean under your eyes," I pointed under my eyes as an answer, and she just giggled and shrugged lightly.

I went off to the washroom, took a bath and freshened up. I went out to see her sitting with breakfast. "Thank God you made it early or I would have eaten all of it... You know I love food," she grinned.

"Yes, I know you are a bakasur." She gasped and her mouth hung open; she threw the brown crust of the bread at me, which I dodged easily.

"What were you writing last night?" I asked her. She looked down at her plate, avoiding my eyes. "Nothing, just writing a few things," she replied.

"Like?" I asked again. She shook her head and looked up, "Personal ones!" She wiggled her eyebrows and flashed her usual smile; I nodded knowing that I would not get any more info from her, and would have to read it myself to know what she had written.

"Watcha doing today boi?" she asked me with a mouthful of bread choking her voice.

"Just sitting with you," I shrugged. She shook her head. "I got movie DVDs from the nurse... It is movie time!" she yelled while throwing her hands up in the air. I smiled at her childish behavior and nodded, "Sure, but first finish your breakfast so that I can go and put the plates out for clearance," I stated. She nodded and continued to eat her food.

"I will just go to the washroom," she said and excused herself, wheeling herself away. I quickly picked up her phone to read what she had jotted on it and opened the notes app. What I saw there almost knocked me down from my chair; it had a note called "Yuvraj" it was the note she had written last night. I opened it and started reading.

13

"I wish I had seen Yuvraj first and not Aarav. I used to pray that things be normal between me and Aarav as a couple always and used to think that we loved each other. This was not the real thing though; we were only attracted to each other. Now I pray that Yuvraj and I happen together. Now that I am in such a pathetic condition, with only one leg, I cannot speak out my feelings - the feelings I have for Yuvraj. I can just sit and write things for him, as I cannot even dance now. Here is what I feel -

"You are not mine,
But sometimes
I pretend that
You wish you were.
I create this idea
that you secretly
want me.
And I often forget
it is something that

I have just made up.

That you are not mine and

you do not want me."

This meant that Aanya had fallen for me! I could not even imagine such a thing, and cannot elaborate how happy I felt, that happiness was far far more than the happiness I experienced when I scored full in Economics.

"I am back, Yuvraj!" she entered with a big smile on her face, pushing her wheelchair in. Thank God! I had locked her phone back again when she was opening the door.

"Good! Come." I sat down on the chair next to the bed and straightened the messed up bed sheet. She looked thankfully at me, "What are we going to watch?"

I thought for a while. "P.S. I love you," I said. I had put a slight emphasis on "I love you." She seemed to notice it because she stared at me for a while, but quickly shook her head as if shaking off her thoughts and shifted her wheelchair while looking for the DVD kept in the bag. An awkward silence surrounded us.

I got up noiselessly as I went behind her and tickled her lightly. She laughed, "Yuvraj Thakur Singh! No tickling," she tried to scold me.

"You think I will not, Aanya Saeed!" I said and tickled her again.

"Yuvi no...no...no! Please stop!" she moved the wheelchair all around the room. I ultimately pinned it to the wall, kneeled down to her level and tickled her stomach again. Sometime later, I stopped, but we were still laughing our heads off. I opened my eyes and realized how close we were. My body pressed over her's, our faces just inches apart, our breaths hitting each other, I could smell her rose cologne and hear our hearts beating fast together at a fast yet perfect sync.

She opened her eyes too and stopped laughing. We stared directly into each other's eyes, scanning the beauty of the other person, occasionally looking at each other's lips.

My emotions were like fireworks and before I could realize it, our eyes were closed and both of us were leaning in towards each other. Finally, my lips touched hers. The warmth of her mouth sent an electric current running through my body. It was some sort of magic, the way her lips connected with mine. Somehow, it felt to me as if the entire world had stopped just for us. This was fully our moment.

Her lips were soft and it felt good. I knew that we would have to stop some time, but I did not want this moment to come to an end. And, neither did she.

Our lips moved together in perfect sync, fitting together, as my thirst for tasting her strawberry lip balm that I had been longing forever since I had fallen for her, was quenched. Everything felt so right, and somehow, among all of the dizziness and the clinging to her like a lifeline, something inside me changed, never to be reversed back.

This new feeling could be dwelled upon later, because I did not yet comprehend it fully, but at that moment, I was content to feel her breath come and go with mine. It was beautiful as I was holding her waist, kissing her, and her hands were creeping up my neck, the fingers tousling my hair.

If I could keep a single moment frozen for all time, that would be the one. I became the very air; I was full of stars. I was silence, and I was music, one clear transcendent chord rising toward Heaven. I believed, then, that I would have risen bodily into the sky but for the anchor of her hand on my neck and her round, soft, perfect mouth.

She suddenly became aware of what she was doing, and pulled herself back with a jerk. "Uh... I. Sorry! Um, Excuse me."

I quickly got up and moved away. "Aanya!" I called her because she started moving her wheelchair away.

"I am so sorry Yuvraj," she said, avoiding any eye contact.

"Your wish has come true Aanya!" I blurted out, which made her swing back the wheelchair in utter shock.

"W-what do you mean? What wish?" she asked.

"I've read the note you wrote on your phone last night," I told her.

"Yuvraj! It is a bad thing to read personal things!" she screamed.

"I had to know. Your wish has come true, actually my wish... I love you Aanya. Will you be my girlfriend?" I asked her finally, mustering courage

She shook her head sorrowfully. "You are feeling pity for me Yuvraj and tagging your crush as love. You love me? Yeah right!" she said sarcastically.

"I do! Seriously." I confessed.

"Since when?" she asked.

"Ever since we were in class seventh, ever since we became best friends," I sighed.

She laughed dryly, "Of course! And why didn't you ever tell me?" she asked again.

"I was afraid you would run away from me if I were to say what I wanted to tell you, and then I would lose your friendship too," I said to her.

"You do not love me Yuvi! You are just pitying me because you know no one would like to be with a physically impaired girl, that too a motherless one!" she whined.

I sighed. "If pity was the reason for my love, then I too would have left like Aarav did," I spoke up.

"Are you serious?" she asked me again.

"Yes!" I replied, nodding.

"In that case, ask me out, properly." She crossed her hands over her chest and smirked.

I groaned, "Fine."

I knelt down. "Aanya Saeed, you are the only girl in my life that I have fallen in love with, and I want it to be you only. I had never thought I would be so lucky as to have you in love with me. But God has listened to me and sent you down just for me. If you exist then I do, if you breathe then I do. You know, I used to believe God existed but could never see Him; but in you, I found and saw my God. Now Aanya, will you please become a part of the story of my life by accepting to be my girlfriend, as being a best friend is too old school? Because as a matter of fact, me 6 feet ka tum 5'10 ki. We will make a perfect match," I asked her.

"Yes, you cute and adorable little ass!" she said and cried a little.

"Why are you crying?" I asked her.

"When I hear such an adorable proposal just for me, and not something read from some book, how can I not help crying," she said as she sobbed.

I picked her up again bridal style and made her sit down on the bed. I set up the laptop on the table kept between us and put in the DVD. I quickly sat down next to her; she held my hand."Yuvraj?" she called me. "Aanya," I replied. "I love you," she said in a whisper but I knew that she meant it most sincerely. I kissed her forehead, "I love you too," I replied.

She smiled and blushed, her cheeks going all red, and turned away to hide her face, playing the movie in the meantime, to cover up her shyness. We spent the entire time we had until her operation, watching 'P.S. I Love you' and occasionally kissing each other's hands.

Soon after the movie ended, we drifted off to our own dreamland, holding hands. It was the end of the story of Gerry and Holly, but this was the starting of our story in a completely new way.

"Yuvraj and Aanya! Wake up children; it is already three in the evening. The operation has to start at four!" the nurse shook me while yelling in her high-pitched voice. I struggled to open my eyes. "Huh what?" I asked her.

She raised her eyebrows and tilted her head. "Don't you have to get the operation done?" she asked me while waving her hand in front of my face in an up and down motion.

I struggled to open my eyes. "Oh damn! It is already three? We are so sorry," I apologized and quickly woke Aanya up. "Aan wake up!" I shook her. "Aanya you can walk!" I said.

She instantly shot open her eyes. "Where?" she said in a disappointed tone.

"You will be able to, if you get the operation done." I said and kissed her forehead; she nodded like a child and smiled at me.

She woke up slowly and hung her arms in the air as if wanting me to carry her on my shoulders.

"What?" I asked her. She made a disgusted face. "Am I going to fly and reach my wheelchair kept on the other side of the room?" she asked in an irritated tone. I grinned sheepishly and picked her up bridal style again.

"They are so cute." One of the nurses whispered to the other in hush hush tones. "They belong with each other." The second one replied whilst smiling admiringly at us.

I made her sit on the chair and bent down to kiss her temple, "You know I love you. Stay strong." I smiled at her; she looked up as she nodded. "I love you too," she whispered to me and grinned cutely, crinkles forming by her eyes.

14

After more than three hours in the operation theatre, Doctor Daanyaal Zaid came out. “Yuvraj, she is a very brave girl.” He smiled, “She is still under the effect of anesthesia, and has to sleep it off once she comes out of it. You can see her tomorrow.” He informed me and went off.

It took every bit of the will power in me to stop myself from barging into her room. My phone buzzed, “Hello?” I answered the unknown number,

“Hi Geeko. Adiba here.” Adiba spoke on the other side quietly.

“Hi Adiba. What’s up?” I asked her.

She sighed, “Just called you know, to know about Aanya. How has she been doing?” She asked quietly, this side of her was totally unknown to me.

“She is doing okay right now; the operation just got over a little while back and was successful,” I told her,

I heard her sigh, “I just wish for her well being. She has done things for me that I will never forget.” She was hinting about the little dating time we shared that Aanya had set up.

"She is with me now." I smiled, I could imagine her gasping,

"Really? You and Aanya? Congratulations gee... Uhm, Yuvraj." She cut herself down by saying Yuvraj.

"It is okay Adiba. You calling me by my name never sounds good. Geek of the week and Geeko is more the 'Adiba type' thing." I smiled.

She chuckled, "Take care of her and join school as soon as possible, tests are going to start and we will miss you if you get absent Geeko." She chuckled again, "Okay bye." She said and disconnected the call.

A week later

"It takes a lot to stand on an artificial leg after an amputation, yet she did it. Now after we make her practice with it for four to five days you can take her home with you." I stood next to Doctor Daanyaal, outside his office, talking about Aanya's condition as he beamed.

"Err... S... Sir the payment?" I asked him. He seemed to be surprised at my question. "Payment?" he asked me to confirm what I had said.

"Yes sir. For the... Um, you know...operation and everything," I asked him.

Instead of replying he chuckled and patted my shoulder, "You love her a lot, son. Her father could not make it due to the death of Aanya's grandmother. He had to stay back in Delhi for her cremation, but he has sent the money. You need not worry about it," he smiled, informing me and went away leaving me standing there outside his cabin.

I quietly crept inside the room to see Aanya sitting on the bed sideways, legs dangling to the floor. She was trying to stand by herself, I guess. I did not disturb her. She was staring at the floor in full concentration, and suddenly she put all the weight on her real leg, and keeping her hand on the stool next to her, she tried to stand up. Unable to balance on one leg properly, she stumbled and was about to fall when I caught her.

"Aanya!" I exclaimed and made her sit on the bed. She looked angry and disappointed. "What were you doing?" I asked with crossed hands.

"I was going to meet Liam Payne. Want to accompany?" she asked sarcastically.

"Li... Li what?" I tried to annoy her.

"Liam Payne, from One Direction." She straightened up.

"You are going to meet him?" I asked her.

A surprised expression covered her face. "Oh! If I had been going then I would have already run all the way to London, United Kingdom. Here I was just trying to walk by myself." I nodded, "Tell me, tell me, tell me something I don't know, something I don't know. Like who is Harry Styles, what it takes to make you smile, getting you not to treat me like a child...baby!" I sang in a quirky voice while doing girly hand movements. She stared at me wide eyed and cracked up into fits of laughter. "I... I c-can..." (laughter) "Imagine y-you..." (laughter) "dancing with an m-" (huge fit of laughter), "With a mop like Selena Gomez does." She cracked up again.

"You still love me." I straightened my collar.

"No, I don't," she said and stuck her tongue out.

"Oh yeah?" I said.

In reply she nodded, I poured a glass of water and handed it to her, and she raised her eyebrows.

"Take a sip from my secret potion," I said pointing to the glass."It'll make you fall in love," this time with a waist move.

"For a spell that can't be broken one sip should be enough." I widened my eyes and showed 1 with my index finger, my mouth open in a girlish way.

"Girl, you belong to me," I said, pointing at her, "I got the recipe," I said faking an evil giggle "and it's called black magic!" I twirled my finger showing magic with an evil expression. All this I sang in a quirky and thin voice like the singers of Little Mix sounded in this song.

She cracked up into laughter again, "I was like 'what should I do with the water?' and then you started with a straight face, 'take a sip from my secret potion'. Too good man, too good." She clapped her hands and I too joined her.

"Okay fine, now, anything new?" She asked me curiously.

I thought for a bit, "Your grandmother passed away, and due to the cremation and everything your dad won't be here." I told her.

The smile was replaced with a sad face, "Oh Daadi? I couldn't even see her one last time because of this accident. Dad had called me to say that she was ill, and I had told him not to rush back, and to take good care of her, that I would manage fine with the nurses here in the hospital, and you to keep me company. Uhm, okay. What else?"

I had spoilt her mood. "And, we have got good luck wishes from Adiba last night!" I grinned; she furrowed her eyebrows then widened her eyes, "Adiba Malik? From our class?" She confirmed and I nodded.

"New side of Adiba, never thought she would send good wishes to someone." She shrugged.

"Amazed?" I asked her and she nodded with a thoughtful expression.

"Well, you know she was in love with you?" She asked me. "Adiba? Me? Really?" I asked her, and she nodded with a cheeky grin. "Never realized. She is so...not falling in love type." I shrugged, "You never noticed Yuvraj, but she was so loud around you so that you notice her." She laughed and we continued laughing and talking for a long time.

Soon the day ended on a happy note. This one accident had changed the lives of both of us so much.

15

Three days went by. Aanya kept practicing with full concentration and dedication, she could now walk a little by herself; she was still limping but did not give up.

"Are you now able to walk a little?" Doctor Daanyaal Zaid asked her. She looked down at the leg and thought for some time. She looked up and nodded, "I can but I am still limping." Her lips formed a straight, thin line.

"It takes time Aanya. Within a week or two, you will be able to walk. You can go home today. Just please keep walking around a little bit, do not sit and order Yuvraj huh. Do work on your own." He patted my shoulder and laughed as I gave a half smile and looked down. She grinned and nodded, "I will not doctor. How much work will this poor tall kid do?" she giggled. "You are a strong girl," he acknowledged her, "And, you son are a loving boy. Both of you don't leave each other." He smiled and excused himself to get her discharge papers ready. Aanya looked at me, "Not even the Gods above..." she spoke, "... Can separate the two of us." I completed her sentence that was a line of You and I from One Direction.

"All set?" I asked her. She seemed lost in her own thoughts. I shook her hand, "Aanya? All set?" She looked startled. "Huh sorry? What?" she questioned. I sighed, "What are you thinking about?" I asked her. She shook her head again and looked at the ground as if she were dreaming about a completely different world. "Just thinking... How I will face all at school," she sighed. "Like you do daily," I said in a 'what is so new' tone.

"Plch, Yuvraj! I have lost a leg, everyone will be practicing for the dance competition there, Noor and Aarav will also be present, practicing hard," she said thoughtfully. "So what?" I asked her. She narrowed her eyes, "Arre yaar! They will all be there dancing, I will not be able to..." she sighed for what seemed to be a zillionth time since she had entered this hospital.

"You are not going to let Aarav and Noor affect your life, now, are you?" I raised my eyebrows at her; she shook her head. "Good, now pack your things and change. We are going to school directly," I informed her. She gasped aloud. "Directly to school? Why?" she asked me. "Because, Aanya, we have missed school since the last one and a half weeks and it is definitely not a good thing." I said in a 'as a matter of fact' tone.

She sighed in disgust. "You love school the most don't you?" she asked me.

I wiggled my eyebrows with a cheeky grin, "Na, I love you the most." She blushed furiously and I left the room for her to change and also because I had to change into my uniform.

16

I knocked at the door of the ward half an hour later after I had changed and brought our bags.

"May I come in?" I asked her.

"Come in," she said and I entered to see her sitting on the bed, wearing her uniform and tying her ponytail. Once done she turned back. "Feels good to go to school after so long," she said, biting her lips as if embarrassed to admit it. I chuckled. "Told you," I said as I shrugged.

She put her hand up, "Help me down, this bed is too high." She gave an apologetic smiled as I nodded and went up to her. I kept my one hand on the small of her back and holding her right hand with the other, made her get down on her left leg. She lost her balance slightly, and grabbed my collar."Careful,lady." I smirked at her. She scanned my face and realized I was too close; I tried to pull my head back but she pulled me by my collar and kissed my lips leaving the taste of her strawberry lip balm. "I do not have to be as long as you are with me," she said with a smile.

"Ahem ahem," we heard someone clear their throat and quickly straightened up. I made her stand straight and turned back to see Doctor Daanyaal Zaid smirking. "Um, it is time for your discharge. Finish up soon and...come out," he said trying to stifle his laughter as he went off leaving us blushing like tomatoes.

"Hospital is no place for romance," I giggled as I told her. "You are irresistible at times. What can I do?" she held my collar with one hand and crept her other hand around my neck to keep balanced. She pulled me close to her. "I will romance with you anytime, anywhere, in any situation," she whispered in my ear sensuously, the tip of her index finger stroking my cheek. I swear she is the biggest tease. She pecked my lips and started walking away holding on to the bed for support.

"That is it?" I whined like a child.

She turned around and gasped, "Don't you know? Hospital is no place for romance," she imitated me.

"HA HA HA. Very funny!" I said and walked out of the room propping her up against the bed.

Reaching the lobby, I signed the papers, took the health certificates and her belongings and went to the lift, remembering how the first time I had run all the way up because the goddamn lift was fucking slow. I chuckled remembering my situation. She looked up at me, "What is so funny?" she asked innocently.

"Nothing, when I first came to know that you were admitted here, I drove like a mad man all the way here, and ran up all the four stories because the lift was slow in coming down," I laughed to myself again and turned to her. I saw that she was biting her lip and giving me a pensive look. "What is it?" I asked her.

"You are so busy being you that you forget that you are already perfect," she smiled at me.

I put my arm on her shoulder and kissed her forehead. Having her with me somehow felt unreal, magical, a dream, and yet somehow so perfect.

The lift stopped at the ground floor and we went outside; I smiled at the receptionist who also recognized me and smiled back. We went outside. "Stay here, I will get the car here," I told her.

"Car?" she asked me. I nodded.

"Why did you come here by car when Aarav came with you?" she asked me.

I joined my eyebrows together. "No, who said that we came together? He did not even tell me the full thing. He just said that you fell from the train and were in this hospital, and went off. He did not even help to get us our clothes. It was Adiba who helped me with everything." I told her.

She widened her eyes and nodded, "Sorry, I thought the other way around," she grinned cheekily.

17

I went to the parking lot and saw my white Renault Duster standing all alone, covered with dust since it had not been driven for the last one and a half weeks. I mentally made a note of sending it for a car wash and drove it to the door of the hospital where Aanya was standing with her phone in hand.

"Let us go to school!" I yelled in an enthusiastic tone, and she chuckled. The nurse helped her to get into the car, and Aanya handed her a five hundred rupees note.

"Five hundred is not much of a sum, right?" I asked her. She furrowed her eyebrows, "She helped us all these days, and she deserved at least five hundred rupees. Now stop being such a kanjoos okay!" she taunted and put on her seat belt.

I smiled as I shook my head and drove out of the hospital. "Play some songs, Yuvi, it's no fun moving around in a dust covered Duster without any songs. Huh." Saying this Aanya fiddled with some buttons on my music system and ended up playing 'Main Hoon Hero' from 'Hero' by Salman Khan. "Aakhon ke panno pe…mene likha tha sau dafa…" she started singing in her bad voice.

"You sing so badly Aanya," I laughed at her.

"Achcha? Right, you are the only Arjit Singh right?" she said in her sassy and trashy way.

"No baby! Only Jagjinder Joginder," I said to her knowing that she would yell at me for calling myself that.

"Oh please! Jagjinder Joginder is only Shahid Kapoor from Shaandaar okay!" she yelled pointing at me, being extremely possessive about Shahid Kapoor.

"Okay fine! Only Yuvraj Singh," I wiggled my eyebrows, "You are not," she rolled her eyes.

"Oh come on stop lying. Am I not Yuvraj Thakur Singh?" I gasped dramatically and she rolled her eyes, again.

"I feel that I am in love," she said in a thoughtful way suddenly.

"Who is the lucky guy? Me or Shahid Kapoor?" I furrowed my eyebrows at her.

"Shahid Kapoor is already my love," she replied.

"And married also? To Mrs. Mira Rajput...oops... I mean Mrs. Mira Kapoor," I said putting too much stress on 'missus'.

She stared at me and groaned. "Can you please stop reminding me that Mira Rajput is now Mira Kapoor and that Shahid is no more single, and help me get over him!" she said in an irritated tone.

"Sorry sorry. Who are you in love with?" I asked straightening my collars.

"I have been with him ever since I was given a phone but I feel for him now," she said and I frowned while thumping my foot on the brake, nearly killing both of us.

"Who is it?" I yelled.

"This emoticon," she said and showed me the disgusted expression emoticon that also has a smirking version of it. I looked up at her, and she laughed. "You can use it and show your non interest clearly," she giggled that I had made an absolute fool of myself.

I shook my head in disgust and drove off to the school; I parked my car and helped Aanya out. She and I walked together to the door when she stopped midway. "Um c-can I go home?" she asked me.

"Why so?" I asked back.

"I feel out of place," she sighed.

I shook my head from side to side, and gently dragged her in.

As we had not had any breakfast at the hospital, we went to the canteen first instead of to the class. I found a booth for both of us and made her sit down. People were giving us awkward and surprised stares as they whispered weird things about both of us together and her accident and that she could never dance again.

I turned back and gave them a cold glare as I went to the food stall to get something for both of us. "Two cheese sandwiches, two black coffees and a bottle of water," I placed the order and took the tray. I turned back and saw Aanya standing near our booth talking to Aarav, anger written clearly on her face.

"What happened?" I asked as I reached them.

"You stay out of this and away from her, get that?" he snapped angrily at me.

"Oh yes! You have only to say so, and I will," I said sarcastically and turned towards Aanya.

"He is sorry for what he has done and when he saw both of us together he realized how much he loves me and wants me back." She said this with a disgusted expression and in a plain voice devoid of all emotion.

"So? Are you going to accept the apology?" I asked her, looking down because I was really afraid that she would say yes. But she turned to me with a surprised expression, "Do I appear like a mad woman? No, right? So why would I accept his stupid, fake and meaningless apology? He left me all alone in the hospital once, when I was in serious trouble; he can do it again. Sorry, but I love you and I am not going to go back to him." She said all this very loudly so that everyone around us could hear and held my hand firmly.

Angry and irritated by the humiliation he faced Aarav got up from his knees. (The stupid moron had been pretending to plead with her on bended knees.)

"You are going to help her walk; it is very good...and keep on doing charity like this. However, did you just realize that she loves dance and that her name is enrolled for the international dance competition that is to be held next week? I challenge you, you motherfucking asshole! Go and try to make this limping, physically handicapped girl dance and win. I challenge you to win the competition against Noor and me. She and I have been practicing for the last two weeks; I will not let you win." He yelled at my face, "Speak up! Will you make it? Or will you back out like a coward?" he asked me. I felt Aanya stiffen under my touch at his challenge and the fury in his words.

"No no Yuvi please. We will not," she whispered to me.

"We will." I saw Aanya's head jerk towards me, "I accept your challenge; I will take part with Aanya in the international dance competition against you, win it and go to The Eternity Dance Troup London with her as a winning student. Mark my words, I will not back out." I spoke loud enough for each and every student sitting in the canteen to hear, but what I heard was Aanya face-palming. "What the fuck on Earth are you even doing Yuvraj Thakur Singh?" she whispered to me in anger and irritation.

"Let us go! I want some positivity at this moment," I said as I held her and took her away with me leaving behind a confused, irritated and annoyed Aarav.

"What the hell was that Yuvraj?" she asked me as soon as our toes felt the air outside the canteen.

"We will take part," I told her. She gasped. "But how? I am not able to walk without your or the wall's support. How the heck will I dance on the stage?" she freaked out.

I sighed, "You will dance and I will be by your side," I told her as I looked into her eyes.

"B-" she opened her mouth but I cut her off.

"We will dance together at the competition and win it together Aanya," I said to her.

Aanya

"We will dance together at the competition and win it together Aanya," he said with so much trust in his eyes, there was something about the way he believed in me that made me believe in myself, and I feel that it is not so hard when he is around. Without even realizing my actions, I nodded and agreed to what he said even though something deep inside me knew that it would be near to impossible.

"Let us go, select the dance, choreograph and then practice very fucking hard. One week is all that we have to polish ourselves," he said in a worried tone. I nodded and went with him to the rehearsal hall.

As I set my foot in the rehearsal hall, memories of me dancing there flashed in front of me. I touched the mirror and remembered the Bharatanatyam dance I did here in front of Noor and Aarav to prove myself - my last dance. I could feel tears welling up in my eyes, blurring my vision; I took a deep breath and wiped them off. No, I will not cry, I will dance.

"Aanya!" Yuvraj's voice from the other end of the room startled me and broke my chain of thoughts. I turned around. "Come, select the song." He patted the chair next to him, I nodded and sat down.

After loads of arguments, laughter, and time, we agreed upon doing lyrical and contemporary on 'Hasi Ban Gaye' from 'Hamari Adhuri Kahani'. Now came the tough part, practices.

After watching a few YouTube videos, we learnt the steps, not easily, I must say. I fell, stumbled and cried for what seemed like zillions of times. However, every time Yuvraj stroked my hair, made me stand up and dance again. We did our practices for the whole of the week, without differentiating between day and night.

18

Finally the day arrived, the day of the competition. The judges entered, Lauren Gottlieb in a golden, shimmery dress, Danielle Paezer killing it with a sober little black dress and Andrew Bartee looking handsome in a dark blue suit, and took their seats with regal elegance. Most of the girls swooned over Andrew Bartee who just remained calm and poised, while the boys had a gala time checking out Lauren and Danielle who were throwing flying kisses to a few.

"It is great to be here and to audition students from St. Laurens' and other schools. Feels as if I am on the sets of Jhalak Dikkhla Jaa." Lauren said laughing at the name of our school, which was the same as hers.

Ronit and Aisha were the first ones to go on the stage. They did a beautiful Kathak performance on Ore Piya from Aaja Nachle, where Ronit played the role of Krishna and Aisha became Radha. As they were already a cute couple, their dance looked very beautiful. Both of them wore bright colors of red and yellow to complement the characters they were portraying.

Next were Shreya and Rajat who did a sensuous tango on Arre aao na from Haider by Shraddha Kapoor. It looked as if a fire brigade should have been informed; their performance was so hot and sexy. Shreya wore a red and black, backless, tight dress ending above her knees while Rajat looked a killer in a black tuxedo.

The next participants after Shreya and Rajat were Noor and Aarav. They both did a typical Bollywood dance performance on Sari Ke Fall Sa from R... Rajkumar. Noor looked okay-okay in a purple sari and Aarav looked absolutely ridiculous in a flower printed orange and green shirt. They tried to recreate the look of Shahid Kapoor and Sonakshi Sinha, but failed to do so because nobody can look better than Shahid Kapoor and also because Noor danced badly that day.

A while later after the other school students had performed our names were announced; I took a deep breath and closed my eyes to control my super fast heartbeat, and then stepped up on the stage with the support of the podium. The thundering applause of the audience was suddenly stilled and there was dead silence, as if a dead body had been sent up and it had revived. I think I saw Andrew gasp, and Danielle asked him not to give such reactions, while Lauren stared at my artificial leg.

All these various reactions took place as we entered on to the stage, and they saw my condition, and doubtless felt sympathetic; that was pathetic – I didn't want anyone's sympathy. I grew nervous with all eyes on me, but instead of showing it to the audience, the judges and fellow participants, I tried to ignore the stares we received - actually, what I received. I looked towards Aarav and Noor, giving them an evil and challenging smirk. At last, Yuvraj and I took our places as the spotlight embraced us and we waited for the soft flow of music to begin.

Once it started with the slow and soothing voice of Ami Mishra, we took a step forward, hand in hand and bowed down towards the audience. We circled each other, our gazes never breaking and I did not even want it to. Yuvraj placed his hand on my back, my hand on his shoulder, and our free hands finally met. I could feel him press it tightly in a reassuring way, as if telling me to stay strong. I looked at our hands and then at him. "I love you" he mouthed slightly and winked.

Together, we danced to the soft and beautiful music, our feet in slow but perfect sync to the beating of our hearts. As the song progressed, I felt as if it was the best day of my life and grew incredibly happy and complete, so I allowed a small smile to play on my lips, seeing which a half smirk broke on Yuvraj's face too. Sudden realization hit me and I understood that we were perfect and made for one another for all time to come. He had worn a white spotless net shirt through which I could see his chest; it was nice how it matched my white, sweetheart neck dress and I felt us as one.

His eyes, green as leaves covered with dew on a cold, winter morning, were deep and irresistible. One thing was for sure... I was one lucky girl to have him as a partner in this dance and in my life. The stare of his deep green eyes burned under my skin and he became like a tattoo - sometimes painful - but I became addicted to the way he felt towards me.

He turned elegantly, his body in tune with the subtle music; we parted away for me to twirl into his arms back. All of a sudden, I lost my balance and made a mistake. I was nearly going to stumble down and embarrass both of us, but he prevented this from happening as he held my hand and made it look as if we had done a step, and I have to say it looked very beautiful, as if it had been practiced for a long time. Coincidentally, I had slipped on "Haan hum badalne lage, girne samhalne lage", and that made it look like a step. Even though I had ruined a little of the sink, I did not quite care at that point of time as I had found my sense of home in his arms and not in London, and to be honest I wanted Yuvraj more than ETD. The warmth between us grew more and more powerful as each second of the song passed. My heartbeat was growing steadily along with it. Our dance was almost perfect; everything from our breathing to how our feet moved stayed in sync, as he was slow for my sake. If, after this very second I were to be called by God, I would not regret it and ask for me to survive, but go away in peace, as I had lived my happiest moment to its fullest.

Yuvraj held me and guided me across the dance floor as if we were in a dream. He kept his eyes on me, yet still, he knew exactly where to take me. Every moment, every angle seemed to be planned in advanced. Nothing felt forced; I literally thought I was floating. Every time our bodies nearly touched, I could feel his hot breath on my cheek and an electric current ran through me. I loved the way in which he towered over me. He was alert, eyes scanning the floor ahead of him, watching the steps, cautious not to step on either of my legs, but was constantly aware of what was happening in his arms. He treated me with respect, as if I were a princess and he was my prince, never forcing movement from me as he knew that right now I could not dance as much as I used to before, but following me through every movement. If he led a step or a pattern and I interpreted the movement differently from what he had intended, he adapted to me rather than forcing change from me. I had a sense of security and safety, knowing I could fully depend on him.

"Yuvraj," I whispered, "everyone is looking at us."

He squeezed my hand slightly and smiled. "Really," he chuckled softly in a sarcastic way, "I have not noticed. I am too busy looking at you."

With that, I definitely knew. He need not say anything more. My heart, my whole being was now his and his alone.

That was the moment when I decided to let go - let my worries, my pain, and anger fly out of the window. Right here, right now, I was living. Nothing else seemed to matter anymore; I allowed him to take me anywhere he pleased on this dance floor. He went right, I went right. He sped up, I sped up. We became one with the song, with the dance and with each other. We continued like that until we had to separate, though I was sad to be away from his warmth. When the song ended, the audience's applause filled our ears. I could not help but smile at him. At that very moment, I wondered how I could not see him before. Yuvraj was the one for me. In my eyes, and because of that dance, I could see how perfect he truly is.

We stood straight as other participants made their way next to us, and waited for the judges to comment on our performances. As Yuvraj held my one hand and the other shoulder, from behind me I could hear him murmur Hanuman Chalisa.

Lauren cleared her throat. "Okay, so I would start with Ronit and Aisha. You people were beautiful, your expressions were amazing and elegance was full on, but you know the beats were a little out of place. Otherwise it was a bang on." She smiled at them and they nodded sadly.

"Next is Shreya and Rajat, ooh la la! What a hotshot performance it was! You guys set the stage on fire!" she said as the crowd applauded.

"Moving on," she sighed sadly, "Aarav and Noor, I love that song and I love its choreography. I know you guys tried to recreate the song but I am sorry to say that you just could not do it." She made a disappointed face.

Next, she smiled at us and our heartbeats rose. "Aanya and Yuvraj," she said and the crowd cheered and clapped instantly, "See! You guys have created hysteria!" she said and stood up giving us a standing ovation. "Enough said," she clapped for us. "How do you do that? Are you a couple?" she asked me as we both blushed and nodded. "You both are incredibly cute! Stay together and God bless you. I pray I get a boy as good as Yuvraj," she said and smiled at us.

Andrew just stood up and gave us a standing ovation. "This girl is an inspiration. Incredible, both of you!" He said and sat down. "Sir no comments?" the host, Josh Desire, asked him. He widened his eyes, "I gave them a standing ovation, dude!" he said as the crowd clapped wildly. Moving on from us, he killed the reputation of Aarav and Noor by saying, "Why did you guys even take part? To make absolute fools of yourselves?" he asked in disgust.

Danielle smiled at us. "If they do not select you, then you are coming in my dance troop. You both are gold!" she smiled at us and clapped. She looked at Aarav and Noor, "I do not want to even comment on your performance. It was not anywhere near ETD's standard." She said this with a stiff expression and sighed.

The hosts, Ashley Brooks and Josh Desire, went to the judges and took the envelope in which they had written the winning couple's name. They both turned towards the crowd, "Who is the winner?" Ashley yelled.

"Yuvraj Aanya..., Ronit Aisha," the crowd was divided into two.

Josh took a deep breath, "And...the winners of Eternity Dance Troup audition and the ones who get an admission at ETD London...are..." he gave a big pause.

"Yuvraj and Aanya," Yuvraj whispered with eyes closed, which meant that he was praying.

"Ronit and Aisha...not you...the winners are Yuvraj and Aanya!" he yelled at the top of his voice as crackers exploded in beautiful colors above us and we stared at each other with surprised expressions.

"These two are now, officially, students of Eternity Dance Troup London!" he yelled again and I said nothing, but jumped into Yuvraj's arms.

"I told you we would win," he whispered in my ears. I sobbed, as my heart was flooded with happiness, and nodded. "Please come up on the podium and say something." Ashley had a big smile on her face as she spoke.

Yuvraj

"He made me open my eyes. He is the best thing that has ever happened to me. Amidst all the bad things that I have gone through, he has been by my side, holding my hands firmly and preventing me from collapsing. He is the one who puts stars in my sky." Aanya flashed her beautiful smile standing on the podium.

I opened my eyes to see people staring at me wide-eyed in pin drop silence.

"This is how it all started and we reached here," the words had not rolled out of my mouth when the sound of clapping filled my ears and she gave me a big hug. "I am so happy to be with you," she whispered in my ears.

"Now I would like to request the winners Yuvraj and Aanya to please come up and accept their admission letters. Along with them I would call upon stage the runners-up Ronit and Aisha to get their certificates," Josh declared and it seemed as if the crowd would never stop clapping.

Epilogue

5 Years Later

Yuvraj

"Three…two…one…turn!" I saw Aanya staring at the mirror and trying to perfect her steps, as she was now able to walk as well as all other people. She wore a navy green off shoulder crop top that revealed her belly button and black leggings with blue denim sneakers, and was dancing to Sun Saathiya from ABCD2.

I sneaked up behind her, "Aanya?"

She swung around, dripping with sweat. "Hi," she breathed. "Let us go home now, that's enough practice for today," I pulled her.

She nodded and walked out with me as we both now lived together.

Next Morning

Aanya

I woke up to the sound of some door closing; I turned to my right to wake up Yuvraj but did not find him. He must have woken up, I thought. As I turned to my left, the sight that met my eyes made me smile broadly; he had made breakfast for me. I saw a delicious treat of donuts, coffee and bread. I smiled at the spread until my jaws hurt.

As I got up and put on the leg, I saw something on my left hand, which made me rub my eyes and look at it again. I brought my hand closer to my eyes. I saw something that shocked the living shit out of me, I stared at it, wide eyed with my jaw practically dropping to the floor and eyes popping out of their sockets, and it was…a…ring! I jumped up on my legs and turned towards the tray with food; it had a note attached to it. It said, "Hi, beautiful. Will you marry me? Please! Love you, Yuvraj xx."

I rubbed my eyes and reread it. I wasn't dreaming, this had actually happened. "Yuvraj Thakur Singh!!!" I yelled at the top of my voice. "Yes, Aanya Thakur Singh?" he came into the room with a smirk.

"This is not a funny prank, Yuvraj!" I warned him.

His smile grew, "And what if I tell you, this ain't a prank?" He asked me. I stared at him.

"Y-you…you wanna…m-marry me?" I asked him, I stammered because I was really shocked at his gesture.

Instead of answering, he knelt down. "Aanya Saeed, you're the only girl who has ever brought me down on my knees… twice. I know you find me kiddish and not a serious person, but I'm sorry, I'm grown up enough to realize that you, my girl, are the one for me. You're that perfect girl for me; you are my dream, the only wish I cannot exchange the world for. Aanya, you put stars in my sky! You made me who I am, and holding you in my arms is more natural to me than my own heartbeat. You deserve the very best, someone who will back you up without limits, let you grow without borders, and love you without end. Will you let me be the one? In short, will you marry me, Aanya?" I stared at him with a happy-surprised-shocked-confused-delighted expression.

"Speak," he shook me as he hissed at me.

I opened my mouth but no words found their way out of my mouth, I grew red as tears of joy flooded my eyes. "This ain't a joke?" I whispered, confirming and sniffing.

"Never will it be," he shook his head from side to side. "Please reply, Aan, my knee is hurting!" he pleaded.

Suddenly all his actions connected. He had got up early just for making my proposal special.

I crossed my arms and pretended to be thinking, even though I knew the answer.

"Aanya Saeed, will you be my Aanya Thakur Singh?" he asked me, yet again.

I smiled at him and nodded, "Yes."

I sniffed as he got up and pulled me in for a kiss, just like the one we had shared for the first time, in the hospital, four years back...